I0569796

TERI BARNETT

Mystics ARE MURDER

BIJOUX MYSTERY SERIES: BOOK 2

Mystics are Murder
Bijoux Mystery Series: Book 2
Published Internationally by Teri Barnett
USA
Copyright © 2021 Teri Barnett
teribarnett.com
Lucky Crow Press

Exclusive cover & interior design © 2021
Indie Book Designer

PRINT ISBN 978-1-7328138-8-5
EBOOK ISBN 978-1-7328138-9-2

Editor: Joanna D'Angelo

This is a work of fiction. Names, characters, places, and incidents are either the product of the author's imagination or are used fictitiously, and any resemblance to any person or persons, living or dead, events or locales is entirely coincidental.

For Black Cat Lou, OG Kitty, Best Cat Friend, inspiration for Griselda

and

Raven, my Mystical Bird Sister

ACKNOWLEDGMENTS

Thank you…

Indiana Writers' Workshop, for your critiques, support, and community over the years. I appreciate all of you.

Joanna D'Angelo, for your amazing editorial work, eye for detail, and continued vision for this series.

My family. You inspire me daily.

CONTENTS

CHAPTER 1

"TELL ME." The customer scooted his chair a little closer to the table. "What do you see?"

Madame Edna Marisol swiped at the mosquito buzzing at her right ear and bristled. She was still working on getting a vibe on this guy and he was already demanding answers. "Please. You must give me a moment." She gestured at the deck of tarot cards in her left hand. "I haven't even laid the cards out yet." The psychic handled the deck, squaring up the edges, then placed the tarot cards in the center of the small round table, face down. "Information isn't always readily available." She forced a smile. "It can take time to get to the heart of things."

"You advertise yourself as a medium." He gestured broadly at the room. "I mean, look at all of this. You have a reading area set up in the back of a nineties Ford panel van with a purple wizard painted on the side of it, for God's sake. If that doesn't scream psychic, I don't know what does." He leaned back against the metal folding chair and crossed his arms, hugging them tightly against his lean frame. "I'm already getting disappointed. Not with the presentation, mind you. The white twinkle holiday lights, green shag carpet, and candles create quite an atmosphere." He glanced around. "So does that huge black cat over there."

"Griselda."

"Whatever."

Griselda hissed and twitched her tail.

"Is that even a house-cat?" He wrinkled his nose. "It's huge, looks like a black mountain lion."

"She's part Maine Coon. They're not known for being dainty."

Marisol held her hand out toward the cat. Griselda ignored it and licked her own foot.

"Well, I don't like cats. Maine or otherwise." He stood and, fidgeting, nearly knocked his chair over. "And this conversation is tedious. Do you have any actual information for me? Or should I move along?"

Marisol looked up at the man and considered him for a moment. High strung, curious thing he was. Though dressed well enough in clean dark blue jeans and a denim button down shirt, his neat appearance was definitely covering up some peculiar streak. She sighed. Oh well, he wasn't her first weirdo client and likely wouldn't be the last. She *was* in the business of fortune telling, after all. And, while the idea of getting your future foretold appealed to most only on a surface level, it did bring out a high percentage of odd folks looking for definitive answers to their haunting life questions and situations. Even she had to admit, though, this one here seemed a little more agitated and stranger than most.

She briefly considered sending him packing, then inwardly shook her head. No. She would not be daunted. She was the Mystical Madame Edna Marisol after all, a professional psychic with over forty years of experience. The show must go on. She wearily waved a hand over the card deck. The motion sent the candles on the table sputtering and the stack of bracelets on her wrist chiming. "Have you ever had a tarot reading before?"

"Do I look like a rube? Of course, I have."

"Then, as I said — and you should already know — sometimes it takes a few minutes for the information to come through. You only just finished shuffling the cards, after all." Marisol pointed at his chair. "Please, sit, relax, and I'll continue." She rubbed her eyes behind her round, gold wire rim glasses and checked her watch. It was past ten p.m. and it had been a long day of travel to get to Bijoux, Michigan from Cleveland, Ohio for the First Annual 'Walk into the Light' Psychic Gathering. She'd only just gotten her little caravan set up at the local Lac Voo Nature Preserve campground when this guy came knocking at her van's back door. She should've followed her gut, just ignored him, and gone to bed. But, money was money, and she had travel expenses to cover.

He dropped back into the chair. "Fine. Fine. What did you say your name was again? I'm trying to decide if I've met you before."

Not a chance. You, I'd remember, she thought, but replied, "Madame Edna Marisol." She forced a smile, picked up the cards, and began laying them out in a traditional cross pattern, chanting softly as she placed each one. "Here at the center is you, the querent. To the left is the past, to the right is the future. Love is above you and the world, below you. These four on the far right represent your challenges, hopes, and fears." She held up one final card and laid it across the center querent card. "And this represents your current challenges." When complete, she put the balance of the deck face down and rested her elbows on the table. "Now, what exactly is it you wish to know? What questions do you have?"

He snorted. "Like I said, this isn't my first time so I'm not going to start telling you things. I know some of you read body language and such." He leaned forward in his seat again and the candles cast shadows around his high cheek bones. "You tell me."

Oh. He was going to be one of *those* clients; someone who wanted to challenge her gift. She dropped the last remnants of formality. "Look, Mister, I'm tired. I've been traveling all day and I only agreed to do this reading after hours because you offered me two hundred dollars. Speaking of which..." She held out her hand and wiggled her fingers until he placed four crisp fifties in it. She counted the bills, then tucked them into her bra strap.

"I've paid you. Now. Seriously. What do you see?"

Marisol squinted at the man, then studied the cards. She picked up the current challenge card. It was the Tower, a card based on the destruction of the Tower of Babel. Beneath it was the Nine of Swords, a man sitting on his bed, head in hands, with swords hanging on the wall next to him. "Something disturbs you. It's keeping you awake at night." She waved the Tower card. "Combined with this, I'd say there's been a huge disruption in your life."

Eyebrow raised, he nodded slightly. "Okay. Go on."

Usually, clients were a whole lot chattier and you could sort of figure out what was bothering them from the conversation. This guy was hanging true to his word, though, and wasn't going to help her out at all. Good thing she could actually read the cards. She knew some of those 'psychics' he referred to who relied completely on cues from their customers.

"It wasn't recent though. I'd say it's been about six months."

"Huh. Maybe you are the real thing. What do you think this disruption was?" He picked up the Tower card and studied it, then placed it back where it was in the spread.

Marisol scanned the layout. Ah. She pointed at the card representing the past. "The Lovers tell me it's a broken heart. Your partner left you for another."

"Wow. You could not be more off base on that. Maybe you aren't so real after all." He pointed his finger at her, like he was holding a gun, and said, "Strike one."

"I beg your pardon?"

"You're wrong. Strike one."

"O-kay...Let's look at your future, shall we?" She took a breath and allowed her mind to clear, then moved the cards around slightly with her fingertips as she considered them. "Though you have possibly felt disconnected from others, I do see you finding some new friends and celebrating life, possibly even love. The Three of Cups tells me that."

"Do I really seem like the sociable type to you?" He pointed at her again. "Strike two."

"I'd appreciate it if you'd stop pointing at me."

He shrugged.

She looked him over. His arms were now crossed and he was sitting back in his chair, leaving his face in shadow. "Well, you *are* closed off right now. So, I suppose, for the moment at least, probably not. And, you know, sometimes people change. The cards are encouraging you to step outside yourself, relax, have a little fun."

"Everything you've told me is surface stuff. Claiming the mantle of psychic," he glanced around the space, "as you have so *obviously* done, I'd think you could go deeper. You know what I'm saying?"

"I do know." Marisol leaned back in her chair and let out a breath. "Tell you what. You come back tomorrow when I'm less tired and I'll do another, full on spread and toss in a palm reading, too. No extra charge."

"How about the palm reading now and then I leave?"

Griselda growled, and he shot the cat a look. "Is that animal dangerous?"

Marisol reached over to ruffle the cat's head. The cat was, of course, just out of arm's reach. She chuckled and shook her head. "Gris likes to think she is. I found her in a campground like this one, probably seven or eight years ago. She walked right up to me and decided I was going to be her human. We've traveled together ever since." She relaxed a little and moved the cards to the side. "Put your hand here, palm up, in the center of the table."

He did as instructed. She brought a candle nearby and studied the crisscross of lines. "I see three or four children. A couple of marriages. Your family of origin was a happy one."

He kept his hand where it was but curled his fingers into a tight fist. "I was hoping you were the one, you know?"

Her eyes met his and a shiver of premonition, like an old memory, ran through her. "Excuse me?"

"The one who would know my secret, who would actually *see and understand* the pain and guilt I carry." In one quick motion, he grabbed the back of her head and yanked her forward. The cards went flying. A candle fell over and the flame went out. A thin stream of wax moved across the table.

Terror filled Edna. She struggled against his grip. Opened her mouth to scream but no sounds would come. Her nightmare. *This was her nightmare!*

Griselda jumped, spitting, and launched herself at the man. The cat landed squarely on his back and he stifled a yell as her claws dug into him. He yanked the animal off with his free hand and, panting, pulled a length of rope out of his pants pocket. He held it poised next to the older woman's cheek and stared hard into Madame Marisol's eyes.

"*You* are not the real thing, Madame Edna Marisol." He flicked the rope. "Strike three."

CHAPTER 2

MORGAN HART, Bijoux's new-ish police captain, walked purposefully into Dave's Deli, a retro throwback diner which had changed little since the fifties. She checked her watch. 7 a.m. Still some time before she was on duty. Not that she was ever really off duty, but it felt good once in a while to tell herself she wasn't working.

She stopped just inside the door and inhaled the familiar blend of aromas — blueberry muffins, cinnamon pancakes, bacon, and, most importantly, coffee.

"Hey, Captain Morgan!" Tom the Cook called out from behind the counter. He snickered and shook his head. "That just never gets old."

Morgan stifled a smile as she shot him a look. The teens in town had started the whole Captain Morgan rum thing when she first arrived and it had stuck. Oh well, she'd been called much worse in her time as a homicide detective back in Detroit. "Yeah. It does. As long as you're there, how about a cup of that coffee?"

"Oh, you just haven't been here long enough," Tom said as he flipped a red ceramic cup over and filled it almost to the rim. "Folks will soon find something, or someone, new to tease. It's only been a couple of months, after all."

She nodded her thanks and took the cup over to a window booth. Morgan breathed in the delectable scent of caffeine, took a sip, and sighed. She'd ventured back to her old hometown of Bijoux on Lake Michigan, when her dad, Able Hart, the former police captain, retired. While she may have only been back for just three months, the fact she had to deal with a murder investigation her first day on the job certainly made it feel a lot longer than that.

Morgan looked out the window and scanned the street. Outsiders were rolling in for the *Walk into the Light Psychic Gathering* being held over the upcoming Fourth of July weekend, so she felt the need to be extra vigilant. Especially since there were no such things as psychics, despite what her dad's girlfriend, Zoe Buffet, claimed. Always the cop. Always observant. Morgan knew it was her job to make sure nothing bad happened around here, including locals and tourists getting bilked.

"How's the coffee?"

She looked up as Jeremy Jones, her tall, solid, red-headed deputy slid into the seat across from her. "Just like the sign says. Best in town, JJ."

"Don't let your dad hear you say that." He picked up a menu and scanned the breakfast choices.

Able had purchased Hal's Hardware store when he retired, and it quickly became the place where the old timers gathered for coffee and gossip. The addition of Zoe's coffee cake day once a month had grown Hal's into the Unofficial Center of the Universe in Bijoux. Morgan looked across the street. A line was forming out the front door of Hal's. "Is it coffee cake day?" She glanced at her smart watch and checked the date. "It's early this month if it is."

"Huh. Does seem early. Maybe Able got in a new batch of paint swatches and they're celebrating," JJ offered. "I think sometimes Zoe looks for an excuse to try out new recipes on everyone." He chuckled. "Not that I'm complaining. She makes a mean coffee cake."

Jerome, the Deli's waiter, strolled over. "What'll you have, Mr. JJ?"

"Give me the Truck Stop, please. Eggs scrambled, rye toast, but no hash browns." JJ patted his belly. "Too many cupcakes from Hannah's shop lately. She brings over the day-old ones and I can't resist 'em. Need to watch the carbs."

JJ's girlfriend, Hannah Bellamy, owned Hannah's Heavenly Confections down the street and her cupcakes were the thing of dreams. "Oh, please," Morgan said. Suddenly self-conscious, she glanced down at her own belly. She *had* loosened her belt a notch since moving here. Maybe she should skip potatoes once in a while too.

As if reading her mind, Jerome said, "Wouldn't hurt you to make healthier choices sometimes, you know. Remember," he pointed his pencil at her, "I see how you eat."

Morgan's eyes narrowed. To hell with it. "Just bring me a blueberry muffin. With a lot of butter. And please top off this coffee."

The server shrugged as he walked away. "Someday you'll wish you'd listened to me."

"So much attitude rolled into that skinny body," Morgan grumbled.

"He just likes to take care of everybody. Remember, it's part of his charm." JJ winked. "Oh, hey Cal. Come join us!"

Caleb Joseph, owner of the local Raven's Nest Bookstore and closeted gothic romance writer, eased into the seat next to Morgan.

"Why couldn't you sit over there, by JJ? Plenty of room on that side."

Cal nudged her with his shoulder. His arm was warm, and the unexpected touch caught Morgan by surprise. She fought the urge to lean into him and stayed where she was, focusing on the handle of her coffee cup.

"Nah. You looked like you could use some company here." Cal grinned at the deputy. "No offense. If you're feeling lonely, I'm happy to move."

JJ laughed and spread his arms across the back of the red vinyl booth. "Yeah, I'm good."

Jerome placed a latte with a swirled whipped topping in front of Cal, a raisin bran muffin on the side. "Your usual," he said, then placed Morgan and JJ's food on the table.

"Thank you, sir. You're the best," Cal said.

"So I keep telling everyone. Let me know if you need anything else."

"What do you have planned for the psychic gathering, Cal?" JJ asked around a bite of egg. "Anything fun or unusual we should know about?"

"I have a guest author flying in from the coast. Picking him up at Cherry Tree Airport later this afternoon."

Morgan leaned back and stared at Cal. "You did not just say 'coast.'"

"I believe I did."

"Are you practicing how to be a hipster now?" She took a bite of blueberry muffin. "Seriously, what is up with you today? You seem awfully happy. You're usually Mr. Dowdy."

"I'm kicking off a new event. Orientation is this afternoon and I'm excited about it. And I am not Mr. Dowdy. I'm Mr. Cool. Ask anyone." He wrinkled his nose at Morgan and pushed up his Ray Ban black horn-rimmed glasses. "I have these. And tattoos. JJ? You going to weigh in?"

"Yeah, you're the opposite of cool, buddy. You still carry that University of Michigan professor vibe. Not that there's anything wrong with that, though Mr. Nerdy is probably more accurate."

"Well, at least I know who my friends are now."

Morgan shoved at him and laughed. "And you know it's us. Only true friends will tell you hateful and honest things about yourself."

Cal looked at her and his dark eyes were like lasers. At that moment, she believed he could see into her soul and she didn't like it. Not one bit. She hadn't felt anything like this since her husband, Ian. Before he was murdered on the job. Damn it, Cal. What was his game today? Morgan shifted in her seat, then did what she did best when uncomfortable and changed the subject. "What else do you have planned for the 'psychic' gathering this weekend?" She made air quotes around the word psychic. "You know, other than your *coastal* visitor."

"Yes, we know you don't believe in such things," Cal said. He continued, "Jack Steve is a renowned psychic in his own right, caters to the rich and famous on the *west* coast, and has written bestselling books about his adventures. He'll be doing a presentation and book signing on Saturday afternoon."

"He has two first names." Morgan snorted. "Who has two first names? Do you think he saw that coming?"

JJ shook his head and groaned. "Cap'n, that was bad, even by your standards."

Cal rolled his eyes. "Other than that, there'll be a psychic fair out in the back yard and on the deck of the shop with readers all day Saturday and Sunday. Tarot, palmistry, numerology, intuitives. You name it, we got it. You should both come over and get a reading." When Morgan groaned, he added, "C'mon, for fun."

"Hannah would like that," JJ said. "She's really into all that stuff, so we'll be there."

"Whatever." Morgan finished her muffin and washed it down with the last of her coffee. Movement on the sidewalk caught her eye. A tall young man, wearing a denim jumpsuit, a black knit shawl around his shoulders, and a plain white turban on his head was hurrying by the window and into the deli. *Psychic Uniform 101?* Morgan wondered.

The man approached their table. "Thank heavens. I just knew I'd find you here."

"Of course, you did," Morgan murmured, taking inventory of the younger man for anything out of the ordinary. His eyes were puffy and tired looking, as if he hadn't slept well, or at all, the previous night. And he was wringing his hands together.

"Can we help you?" JJ asked.

"I'm officially requesting a wellness check. My dear friend and mentor, Edna Marisol – you might know her as the famous Mystical Madame Marisol of Cleveland Circus legend – well, I haven't seen her all morning. And she's not answering her phone or knocks on her van door." He pulled his shawl tight around his shoulders. "I came into town to see if she'd decided to run some errands with one of the other psychics but I haven't found her. I did a tarot card spread about it before I came here. All indicators point to something bad happening."

Morgan shoved Cal out of the booth and stood next to the younger man. All her cop senses were tingling. "Your name is...?"

"Oh. I'm Rocky Banks."

"Rocky Banks? Is that your actual name?"

He huffed. "Rocky is short for Rockefeller. My parents had high hopes for me." He held up a hand and his mala beads clicked together. "Before you say anything, yes they're proud I'm a psychic. We make good money." He frowned. "Well, we do once our mentors set us free."

"Any fancy titles to go along with your name I should know about, Rocky?" Morgan paused. "What exactly is the male version of Madame?"

"I'm sure I don't know." Rocky shrugged. "And I can't claim any titles quite yet, including officially calling myself an honest to goodness psychic. Of course, I have the gift, but I'm still considered in the community to be a bit of a newbie." He pointed at his head covering. "Edna has been mentoring me for the last couple of years. I get a black one when I go out on my own."

Who knew there was a hierarchy in the psychic world? "Tell me about your friend. Edna? Where is she staying?"

"Out at the Lac Voo Nature Preserve campgrounds. There's a group of us there, all in the area near the marshy part." He leaned in and smiled, bringing the scent of patchouli with him. "It's the spookiest spot, you know."

Morgan suppressed the urge to scoff. She still had a job to do, whether she agreed with these beliefs or not. "Is there anything else we should know about this woman?"

Rocky shook his head. "Not that I can think of. Although she does have a large black cat who travels with her. Griselda. I haven't seen her either."

"Okay. Thank you for contacting us. We'll go have a look."

"This really just isn't like Edna. She's quite the social butterfly and is usually up bright and early with a pot of coffee to share with the other campers." Rocky glanced around the table. "Thank you all for your help."

A shiver ran through Morgan as she watched the man leave. Seems nothing good ever happened out at the Preserve. That's where they'd found the body of famous romance author Cecelia Beauregard the day after Morgan arrived in Bijoux, and she didn't like the implication something bad may have happened again. She hooked a finger at JJ. "Come on. Let's go take a look."

"Not gonna let me finish breakfast, are you?" He stared at his unfinished eggs and toast. "You know it's more than likely nothing. Plus, there's the possibility of coffee cake across the street." When Morgan didn't respond, he glanced up. "Oh. You got a vibe."

"I got a vibe."

"Can I just point out the irony?" Cal asked.

"No." JJ and Morgan answered in unison. "Cap gets to have her vibes," JJ continued as they paid and walked out of the restaurant. "It's a cop thing."

"Where do you think you're going?" Morgan asked without turning around, knowing Cal was right behind them.

"I'm going with you, of course," Cal said.

She pivoted as she opened the driver's door on the police truck parked along the curb out front. "No. You're not going with us. This is potentially police business."

"Potential being the key word. C'mon. You know I can be helpful. You practically made me a deputy during the romance writers' conference." He reached around JJ, opened the passenger side door, and slid in.

Morgan put on her silver aviator sunglasses and stared at him over the rim. "Dammit, Caleb. You are not welcome to meddle in police business. We've been over this. Numerous times."

JJ shoved his large frame in, which shoved Cal up against Morgan, and pulled the door closed. "Rangers are not made for three in the front."

"Yeah, no kidding." Morgan sighed. If she'd learned anything since she'd been back in Bijoux, it was that Caleb Joseph was one of the most stubborn men she'd ever met. "When we get there, stay in the truck. Understood?"

"Perfectly." Cal grinned and pulled a small notepad and pen out of his shirt pocket and started writing.

Morgan decided to ignore him. She turned the ignition and pulled out onto Main Street, driving past the fully renovated shops, the partially renovated ones, and the Hold Outs who refused to compromise their "aesthetic" for the sake of progress. Or tourists, for that matter. She'd heard the mayor was going to start cracking down on the Hold Outs.

"What's with the notebook?" JJ asked.

"Don't encourage the man, JJ."

"I'm glad you asked," Caleb replied rolling his eyes at Morgan's comment. "I'm thinking about expanding my genres. Gothic romance will always be my first love, but I've decided to write a mystery. You two are going to be my research for the police investigative portion of the story."

"Oh hell no. That is not happening." She'd had writers ride along

12

with her when she was a homicide detective in Detroit. They were always in the way and, despite all the note taking, still got most everything about her job wrong. "We are not going down that road."

Caleb continued to look straight ahead as he tucked the note pad and pen away.

Well, that was way too easy. "I know what you're doing," Morgan said.

"I put the notepad and pen away, as requested."

"Are you recording us?"

"Geez, Captain Hart. If paranoia had a poster child, it would be you. How about you relax for once?"

JJ glanced over at Morgan, then back out the window. "Careful, Professor. I can see her brain clicking away. She's already calculating how to take you out and hide your body when we get to the Preserve for this wellness check."

Morgan could feel Cal's eyes on her and clenched and unclenched her jaw. *Do not engage,* she told herself, and focused on the tree-lined, two-lane highway stretching ahead.

CHAPTER 3

Twenty minutes later, Morgan turned onto the dirt road leading into the Lac Voo Nature Preserve. It was Thursday morning, and the coming Fourth of July weekend meant the summer season Up North was in full swing. The dune grass was tall and green and tourists were lounging on the beach. Temperatures were holding steady in the mid to high 70s, dipping into the low 60s at night. Despite the warmth, Lake Michigan was her perpetually chilly self.

Morgan drove across the gravel parking lot, turned toward the campgrounds, and pulled into a parking spot near the host site. She shut the truck off and said to Cal, "I know you're not going to stay in the vehicle. Just please don't get in the way in case there *is* something going on, okay?"

"You got it."

She sighed, opened the door, and exited, JJ and Cal following.

The Preserve was populated mainly by the camping psychics and they filled the fifteen camp sites with all manner of vehicles: full size RVs, old Volkswagen camper vans, regular vans, even a couple of motorcycles with those small single campers hitched to them. She made a mental note to look at the bikes later. Might be time to add something a little larger to her motorcycle family. A trailer was oddly appealing, but the vintage Triumph Bonneville she'd inherited from her mom would probably never be able to tow something like that.

JJ and Cal followed Morgan to the picnic table where the hosts were sitting, an older man and woman, maybe mid-late-sixties. "Good morning," Morgan said. "I'm Captain Morgan Hart. This is my deputy, JJ Jones."

"Is there a problem?" the man asked. He wore one of those African dashiki shirts with orange geometric prints all over, faded cut off denim shorts, and a ponytail in his thinning, gray hair.

"Why would you assume there's a problem?"

He and the woman looked at each other and laughed. "Because the pigs are here. That doesn't happen by accident," the woman said.

"Pigs. Nice," JJ said. "You do know people don't really call us that anymore?"

The man shrugged. "Call us anachronistic."

"How 'bout I call you by your real name, Mr...?"

"Rocket. Davey Rocket and this is my soul mate and life partner, Daisy." He leaned across the picnic table and shook their hands. "She prefers to go by only one name."

"Oh-kay. Would you please pull out your roster and tell me where Edna Marisol is parked?"

"That's an easy one." Daisy pointed to the other side of the camp-ground. "See the purple van with the wizard on the side? That's Edna's." Daisy sniffed. "She must be sleeping in today. She's usually up at the crack of dawn, serving coffee and donuts. You'd think *she* was the campground host, not us."

"And that bothers you...?" Morgan asked.

Daisy thought about it for a moment. "Sometimes, but I suppose she does it for attention. Old psychics never fade away, they just keep grappling for the limelight, especially ones used to it like Edna. She used to be in a traveling circus, you know. Back in the day."

"So I've heard," Morgan said.

"It sounds like you didn't like her much," JJ offered.

"I liked her well enough." She turned to Davey, who was rear-ranging his ponytail. "Is there something wrong? Are you getting premonitions?"

Davey shook his head. "Nothing coming through at the moment, just thought I heard a spirit voice." He looked at Morgan and tapped at his ponytail. "It's an antenna to the spirit world."

Honestly, could the conversation get any weirder? Morgan thought. They all stared at each other for a heartbeat before Cal broke the silence.

"I'm Caleb Joseph," Cal said, extending a hand to Davey and then Daisy. "Looking forward to seeing you at the psychic fair. I hope you'll stop in for the book signing and discussion with Jack Steve on Saturday."

"It's nice to finally meet you, Caleb. We're both excited to be here for the gathering. And, we wouldn't miss the presentation. Jack's been a long time favorite of ours." Davey put his arm around Daisy and hugged her to him. "Did you know we were the inspiration behind his second book, *Psychics in Love*?"

Cal slung a leg over the picnic table bench and sat across from the couple. "Really? I thought that was more of an autobiography."

Davey and Daisy looked at each other and smiled. "Yes, *our* autobiography."

"Um, that's not how an autobiography works." He turned to Morgan, but she and JJ were already standing outside Madame Marisol's van. "If you'll excuse me." He jumped up and headed after the officers.

"So, what do you think?" Cal asked.

"You do know we just got here, right?" Morgan shook her head and knocked on the side door of the van. No answer. She and JJ circled the vehicle, finding all the doors locked, nothing out of the ordinary. Then she heard it. The bloodcurdling cry of a hungry cat.

"I'd say the cat being locked up in there is enough cause to open the van, don't you think?" JJ asked.

"Definitely." Morgan knocked on the passenger side window again. Still no answer. "JJ, please get the door opener out of the truck."

He returned a few minutes later with a long, thin piece of flexible steel with a hook on the end. He slid it between the door and side of the van until there was a click.

"Good work," Morgan said. She opened the door and the largest black cat she'd ever seen launched itself at them. She managed to catch it with only a few scratches for her trouble. She held the cat tightly to her chest and ruffled the fur on its head. "You must be the hungry beast we heard. Griselda, right?"

Griselda mewed and flicked her tail. Morgan started to melt.

"Um, Cap. Come take a look."

Morgan snuggled Griselda before reluctantly handing the cat off to

Cal, who immediately started murmuring endearments in a baby voice. "Really?" Morgan said.

He turned and walked away without responding, still whispering to the feline.

"What did you find, JJ?" Morgan asked as she stepped into the van. She immediately stopped at the opening, pulled a pair of black nitrile gloves out of her back pocket, and slipped them on. "Got a pulse?" She asked, already knowing the answer based on the awkward position of the body, skin tone, and bruising around the neck.

JJ shook his head and rocked back on his heels.

Morgan let out a breath and looked around the van. A round folding table was toppled over, dumping tarot cards, candles, and crystals onto the green shag carpet. It was surprising the whole thing hadn't caught fire. The white twinkle lights were still on and cast an eerie glow on who she assumed was the Mystical Madame Edna Marisol. "Go ahead and call Doc McVie, JJ. We can process the scene around the body until he gets here." She started taking pictures with her phone. "Oh, and remind him not to share anything with Connie Graham. We don't need her here stirring things up until we know for sure what happened."

Doctor Fleetwood McVie, whose parents were lifelong Fleetwood Mac fans, was the town family doctor, medical examiner, and mortician. His girlfriend, Connie Graham, was the local TV news reporter, and, since she and Connie were teens, Morgan's nemesis. Connie had the amazingly annoying gift of showing up where she wasn't wanted and was a pro at spreading rumors.

"Hey, did you find any cat food in there?" Cal asked as he walked up. He stopped just short of entering the back of the van. "Is that...?"

"We assume so," JJ said. He stood and looked through a couple of storage lockers built into the side of the van. "Here you go," he said as he pulled a bag of Hungry Cat Mix out and handed it to Cal.

The cat started howling again. They all looked at each other, then at Edna. Morgan walked around the body and let out a sigh of relief. "The cat did not try to eat her."

"Thank goodness. I wasn't sure how to report cat cannibalism," JJ said.

"It's only cannibalism if they're eating their own kind. I don't know what you call cross species munching," Cal said.

"Dinner?" Morgan offered.

Cal shook his head. "I can't believe you said that."

Morgan shrugged and continued bagging and tagging potential evidence: tarot cards, candles, crystals. It looked like a mini new age shop, all in this van. After taking more pictures, she pulled the folding table upright. "Hey, JJ. Take a look at this." Carved into the wax in all caps was the word FRAUD. "This looks like it was written with someone's finger. Please take some pictures and then see if you can get any prints from it." She leaned in and followed the lines with her eyes. Sharply drawn, tight spacing. "Maybe Doc can find some DNA."

"Well, well. Another murder out at Lac Voo Nature Preserve. Death sure does seem to follow you around, Morgan."

Morgan didn't bother to turn around. "What are you doing here, Connie?" She checked her watch. Thirty minutes since they'd arrived. Connie was fast today. "Did you by any chance come with Doc? Him, we're looking for. You, we're not."

"No, that lovely couple over there called me. Something about freedom of the press and the need to avoid any police or government cover-ups." Connie sent Davey and Daisy a finger wave. "If Woodsy's on his way, though, I'll make this fast. That should make you happy, Morgan, not that that's a priority."

"You and Doc on the outs?" JJ asked.

"Let's just say we've hit a rough patch and I've agreed to stay ten yards away from him until we sort it all out."

"I'm sorry to hear that, but not sorry you're leaving. Goodbye." Morgan tried to pull the van door closed, but Connie wedged her foot in. Morgan stared hard at her. "Go away, Connie. I promise we'll let you know if anything nefarious has transpired."

Connie craned her head around Morgan and looked into the back of the van. "From the looks of it, the Detroit Killer is back."

"We've been through this. There is no Detroit Killer. Remember? JJ and I disproved your ridiculous theory when we solved the last case." Morgan shifted again to block Connie's nosy gaze.

"I have it on good authority that case isn't really solved," Connie said.

Morgan straightened. "What are you talking about?"

"I decided to do some research of my own recently and visited with Susan up in Traverse City. She's recanting her confession; said she didn't murder those people. Said you forced her to say she did it so you could solve the case and not look bad, throw suspicion away from the Detroit Killer." Connie gave Morgan the once over. "Which, of course, is not shocking at all to me."

"Wait. You did what?" JJ shook his head. "So not cool, Connie."

"I'm only going to say this once, Connie. It is not your job to get involved in our cases." Morgan stared hard at the other woman. "Especially ones we've already solved."

"And I'm only going to say *this* once. I'm an investigative reporter. It *is* my job to look into murders and such." She angled her head around Morgan. "Like the one right here."

"We're not calling this a homicide until Doc does his assessment."

"I don't see it that way. Like I've said before, death follows you. Like Tippi Hedren in that Hitchcock movie, *The Birds*. Only you're not nearly as glamorous. You're just plain bad luck. You returned to Bijoux from Detroit and this sleepy little tourist town became a magnet for murder." Connie shrugged. "It's a reasonable conclusion to make."

"Only if you're fishing for a story where there isn't one." Morgan gave her a narrow-eyed stare. "Don't you have anything better to do?"

"Reporting the news is my job. There *is* nothing better," Connie said. She waved Maria, her camerawoman, over, who trained the camera on Connie's face. She stood in front of Morgan and began her report. "I'm on the scene with Bijoux's police force at the Lac Voo Nature Preserve where, once again, a body has been discovered. The camping psychics believe it to be one of their own, Madame Edna Marisol, the beloved intuitive and tarot reader of Cleveland Circus fame." Connie shoved the mic in Morgan's face. "Tell us what you know so far, Captain Hart."

Morgan pushed the mic away and turned her back to the reporter. "Go away, Connie," she flung over her shoulder. "You know I'm not ready to make a statement."

Unaffected, Connie continued, "As usual, our dear police captain is more intent on keeping secrets than on maintaining the safety of our beloved town."

"Seriously, Connie?" Cal walked up, still holding the cat who was nibbling chow out of his hand. "You know Morgan does a great job."

Connie eyed him up and down, tapping a finger on her chin. "You moved here from Ann Arbor, didn't you? Perhaps it's not a Detroit Killer. Perhaps we're dealing with an Ann Arbor Killer who followed you here seeking revenge. Perhaps the killer is determined to undermine the former University of Michigan professor by ruining his events. After all, you sponsored the romance writers' retreat *and* this psychic gathering. You are also a common link."

Cal scoffed.

She turned her attention back to the camera. "Dear Madame Marisol, dead at the hands of a killer intent on who knows what? This cozy local campground shaken to its very core. Each and every psychic is running to their tarot cards and crystal balls to determine who could be next at the hands of the Detroit — or Ann Arbor — Killer."

CHAPTER 1

"WHAT DO we have on the docket today?" Doc McVie asked as he walked up to the van. He pushed up his round wire rim glasses. "Murder or natural causes?"

"That would be your decision, wouldn't it?" Morgan said.

Doc bristled. "Of course it is. I still want to know what your initial impressions are."

"Likely murder, based on the scene and positioning of the body," Morgan said as Doc's eyes widened. Morgan followed his gaze and blew out a breath. "The host family called Connie," she ground out.

Connie waved at them.

Doc shook his head, motioned to his assistant, Maggie Cornet, who'd been waiting by the ambulance as he climbed into the van. Maggie hurried over, body bag in hand.

Maggie paused before entering the van. She winked at JJ. "Hey, JJ. How's it going?"

"Would be better if we weren't heading toward another death investigation.'

"True. Things okay at home?"

"Maggie, I need your help," Doc said from inside the van.

Maggie sighed and unfolded the body bag. "We can catch up later," she said with another wink as she entered the vehicle.

"She's still sweet on you," Morgan observed.

"And it's still not mutual," JJ replied.

AN HOUR LATER, Doc and Maggie were headed to the morgue with Edna, the crime scene had been secured, and Morgan drove Cal and JJ back to town. She pulled the blue squad truck up to the curb in front of the police station. Built in the thirties, the building was made of limestone, river rock, brass accents, and maintained a serious Art Deco attitude. It also shared a wall with the Town Hall.

As the trio exited the truck, Morgan said, "JJ, please go on inside and start running searches to see if there are any similar deaths out there."

"You think there might be something else going on?"

"I don't know, I still have a vibe I can't shake and want to make sure we don't miss connecting any dots." She shrugged. "If there *are* any dots to connect, that is."

JJ picked up the evidence box from the back of the truck. "I'm on it. What are you going to do next?"

"I noticed Mayor Ed walking into dad's store when we drove past. I'm going to let him know what's going on. You know how antsy he gets." She checked the time. A couple of hours had passed since Connie left the campground. "It's possible he's already heard about it from Connie, too, and that never goes well."

"It is an election year, you know," Cal said, leaning against the truck bed.

Morgan rolled her eyes. "Yeah, so he keeps reminding me. I hate politics."

Cal pushed against the truck and took a step forward. "C'mon, I'll go with you. Mayor Ed likes me. Maybe I can help cushion the conversation."

"Appreciate the offer, but I'm pretty sure not even a feather bed on a mountain of cotton balls could soften what I have to tell him. Morgan crossed her arms. "Besides, don't you have a bookstore to run? A psychic with two first names to pick up at the airport?"

"I have an intern — you remember Billy Livernois, the graffiti kid? — he's watching the shop for me."

"I think that's great you're mentoring him," JJ said. "These kids around here need all the support they can get."

"He's a good kid, just needed an outlet." Cal glanced at his watch. "But damn. I forgot about Jack Steve. Guess you'll have to continue this investigation without me for the moment." They'd found a cat carrier in the van and brought Griselda along with them. He patted the carrier where it rode, secured, in the back of the truck. "Shall I drop Griselda off at Doctor Pete's for a checkup? Make sure she didn't sustain any trauma?"

Morgan considered him. She already knew he had a cat thing and, if she were being completely honest with herself, she found it kind of endearing. *Oh hell, no.* Everyone likes a person who cares about animals and that's *all* it is, she reasoned.

"I'd appreciate it. Please tell the vet to check for anything unusual. After all, Griselda is our only murder witness. Well, besides the murderer." She blew out a breath. "Assuming it *is* a murder."

Cal sighed. "It's too bad cats can't talk." He pushed his finger through the gate on the front of the crate and patted the animal's foot. "Pete does a great job, but I'll inform him of this kitty's special situation. Hopefully there's nothing more unusual about her other than the fact she has five little toes on each foot." He made clicking sounds with his tongue. "You are obviously a Maine Coon, pretty kitty. Or at least partly."

"Maine Coon?" Morgan froze. How did she miss that detail? She was a cop, after all, trained to notice everything.

"Yes. Just look at these feet." He continued to tsk and click at the cat. "Of course, there are other breeds with five toes, but her other markings and fur sure make it seem likely."

Morgan hesitated. She did love Maine Coons. In her mind, they were the Holy Grail of Cats. And this one here, Miss Griselda, was certainly a beautiful one. She started to reach for the carrier, then held herself back. She had a murder investigation to get underway, not a kitty play date. Though the latter sounded infinitely more appealing. "Okay, thanks for offering to take her over. I'll check in with the vet later," Morgan said as she headed across the street to Hal's Hardware.

"If there's any coffee cake, please grab me some," JJ called after her.

"Me too," Cal said.

Morgan waved her hand. "You both know there won't be any left."

"Well, a man can hope...." JJ said.

GOING into Hal's Hardware was always a step back in time for Morgan. Even though her dad had owned the store for a couple of years now, it hadn't changed since she was a kid and he used to bring her here. Metal shelves with worn blue paint, wide wood plank floor with the finish worn off, the whole place crammed full of anything you could possibly want or need for your next home improvement project.

She heard voices and walked toward the back of the long, double shotgun style building. Standing around, over a coffee bar made from a solid core wood door and a couple of sawhorses, were her dad Able, his girlfriend and local psychic Zoe Buffet, Mayor Ed Peltier who was perpetually running for re-election, and Tut, who owned the motorcycle/scooter repair shop down the street and was on his way out. "Hey Tut, I'm going to need to talk to you about a camper trailer for my bike," Morgan said. He smiled and gave her a thumbs up as he passed by. Tut was not one for mincing words.

"Morgan!" Able said as he made his way around the counter. He hugged her tight, then held her at arm's length. "I know that face. Let me pour you a cup and then you can tell us all about it."

Zoe didn't say a word, just continued to watch Morgan with a keen eye. A shiver ran down Morgan's spine. While she did not believe in psychics, Zoe could be downright creepy sometimes. "Zoe?"

"Morgan?"

"Coffee?" Able said as he handed her a cup.

Morgan stared into the steaming black liquid for a moment, mentally forming her words. Just as she opened her mouth to fill them in on the morning's events, her phone beeped a text message. She pulled it out of her back pocket and read the note from JJ. *Based on a quick database search, this is the third psychic killed in as many months. Still digging in.* Morgan let out a breath and tucked her phone away.

She pushed her choppy brown hair out of her eyes and looked up at the mayor. "You're not going to like anything I have to say right now." Morgan put her cup down. "There's been another death out at the Lac Voo Nature Preserve."

"You're not saying it, but I'm going to assume it was a murder. What I want to know is how is that possible? Didn't you increase the patrol in that area after the last time?"

"JJ and I pull extra shifts when we can, but there are just the two of us, you know? We have to sleep at some point."

The mayor tugged at his shirt hem, something Morgan had come to learn was his 'tell' when aggravated. "Well, this is completely unacceptable."

"Yes, being shorthanded *is* unacceptable. What's even *more* unacceptable is a woman died last night. We're still waiting for confirmation from Doc McVie, but it appears she was strangled."

"You know I meant it's unacceptable with this being an election year."

"I know what you meant. I was helping you not sound so self-centered when we have a woman in the morgue."

Mayor Ed puffed himself up. "Now you see here, *Captain*..."

Able stepped between them. "Let's all settle down." He turned to Morgan. "Do you know who it is? ID'd the body?"

"It's Edna Marisol, isn't it?" Zoe asked.

"How did you know that? Has Connie been on TV with this already?" Morgan asked. "I told her not to report anything until we'd confirmed all the details, not that that ever stops her."

"No. I mean, I don't know. Haven't had the TV on today. It's just, I thought I heard her voice late last night. Woke up straight up out of a dead sleep."

"Probably not the best choice of words, sweetie," Able said.

Zoe pushed a strand of long silver hair out of her eyes. "Oh. Yeah. Probably not."

"Did she say anything to you?" Able asked her.

Why did he insist on encouraging her? "Dad, we've talked about this..."

Able held up a hand. "Not now, Morgan."

"Let me think." Zoe rubbed her forehead. "She was sad, so unhappy. Said something about Griselda. 'Griselda is my key,' I think. No idea what that means other than that cat was her only family." She leveled her gaze at Morgan. "Did you find her? Griselda, I mean."

"I found both Edna and Griselda. Caleb is taking the cat over to the veterinarian for a checkup as we speak."

Mayor Ed interrupted. "Enough talk about cats. What are you doing about this, Morgan?"

"JJ and I have just started our investigation, but you can be assured we'll be thorough. We'll also do everything we can to make sure folks — especially the visiting psychics and end of season tourists — feel safe here. It's Thursday and the event ends Sunday evening, so we just need to get through the next few days with no incidents."

The mayor nodded. "I better not hear anything from Connie Graham that I haven't already heard from you, understood? You keep me informed."

"Every step of the way." *Well, most of the steps.* Some things she wouldn't be ready to share until she'd vetted them, like the possibility of a psychic serial killer on the loose. "I need to head back to the station. Oh, Zoe, I almost forgot. Did you have coffee cake today? We saw the line earlier. JJ and Cal asked me to bring them each a piece if you did." She smiled. "Of course, I told them there wouldn't be any left."

Zoe reached behind the counter and pulled out three small paper plates, a slice of coffee cake on each, and covered with plastic wrap. She handed them to Morgan. "I saved you each a piece."

Morgan lifted the edge of the plastic and inhaled the rich, buttery cinnamon scent. "What's the occasion? You're off by about a week."

Zoe looked over at Able. He leaned on the counter and reached for Zoe's hand. "We're getting married."

Morgan stared at both of them. "What?"

"Isn't it wonderful?" Mayor Ed said as he left the store. "I'll leave you three to your family moment."

"Coward," Able called after him, laughing.

"And you were going to tell me when?" Morgan asked.

"Today. We just decided last night the timing was right." Able squeezed Zoe's hand. "You could say the stars all aligned, what with so many of Zoe's friends in town this weekend."

"I hope you can be happy for us," Zoe said.

Morgan shook off her initial astonishment. Even though her mom and dad had been divorced for over twenty years, and her mom lost her fight with cancer three years ago, it was still a bit of a shock. It didn't matter he'd been with Zoe for a few years now; to think of her dad with someone else was still plain weird in her mind. But, as a reasonably functioning adult, that was her issue to parse through, not Dad's or Zoe's. *Life goes on, right?* "Oh, goodness, of course I'm happy for you! It's just a surprise." She hugged them both. "Please let me know if I can help with anything."

"You're going to be busy with the investigation," Able said.

"I know. But I'll make it a point to carve out some woman time to shop or whatever, if you need me, Zoe. Or man time, for you Dad. Whatever I can do."

"Thank you, Morgan. I'll let you know," Zoe said, reaching for Morgan's hand and giving it a gentle squeeze. "My sister, Rennie, is in town for the gathering so maybe the three of us can at least grab tea and cupcakes over at Hannah's and chat about some details."

"I'd like that very much." Morgan smiled, then grew serious. "I wish I could stay, but I need to go get this investigation underway. Honestly, I thought I was putting murder behind me when I left Detroit and moved to Bijoux." She shook her head. "I couldn't have been more wrong."

CHAPTER 5

"WHAT DO you have for me, JJ?" Morgan asked as she closed the station door behind her.

JJ looked up at her from his computer monitor and shook his head. "Nothing new since I texted an hour ago." He leaned back in his chair and crossed his arms. "Two other psychics killed in the last three months. How weird is that?"

Morgan perched on the edge of JJ's desk. "What are the locations?"

"First one was in Traverse City. Second, Detroit. Now here. No real pattern, just a bit of a zig zag around the state."

Morgan stood and walked over to the Michigan map hanging on the wall. She placed a red pin in the three spots and considered them. "Well, it does make a 'V.' Other than that, I got nothing." She rubbed her chin. "Any other psychic fairs going on in those areas at the time of the murder?"

"Ah. Good thought. Let me look into that," JJ said, swiveling around in his chair.

Morgan's phone pinged. A text message from her ex-partner in Detroit Homicide, Elizabeth Shore. Perfect timing. She looked up at JJ. "Thanks, JJ. I'm going to call Liz and see if she can tell me anything about their dead psychic."

Morgan hit the call button on her phone and stepped into the alleyway next to the police station.

"That was fast," Liz said. "Is it really that slow in Bijoux?"

"I wish. Just had another murder turn up out at the nature preserve. We're waiting for the M.E. to confirm, but when you've been working homicide as long as we have, you just know."

"I do know. And wow. I thought Bijoux was a sleepy little beach-side town. What is going on there?"

"It's just plain crazy. Another event – hosted by Caleb Joseph, of course - and another murder." Morgan rubbed her eyes. "I'm beginning to wonder if I *am* some sort of jinx. Or if Cal is."

"You're more of an acquired taste than a jinx. And from what you've said about Cal, he just seems more cute and annoying than a lure for a killer." Liz said.

"I never said he was cute. Just annoying."

Liz laughed. "You didn't have to, I could hear it in your words. It sounds like that reporter of yours is blaming you again."

"She's not mine. And yes, she keeps yammering on about the hunt for the 'Detroit Killer.' And she's now added 'Ann Arbor Killer' to her menu of misinformation." Morgan sighed. "Speaking of which, our research shows a psychic was murdered in Detroit last month. Did you happen to catch that case?"

"Actually, yes, my team is working on it."

"Anything you can tell me about it? I'm trying to connect some dots, if possible."

Liz didn't answer right away, so Morgan knew she was choosing her words carefully. While she and her former partner always brainstormed ideas, they also worked hard to keep overzealous conjecture out of their investigations.

"Look, I understand if you don't want to make too many assumptions, probably more than most. But the woman killed last night was a psychic as well. And there was another psychic killed about three months ago up in Traverse City, but you probably already knew that. If it's the same person, they sure as heck are getting around."

"And we have a pattern of behavior. Going after people who predict the future. Possibly an axe to grind because they want a different outcome than they're being told," Liz suggested. "That's about as far as we've gotten."

Morgan snorted. "Aren't all fortunes the same? They wave a hand, deal some cards, and suddenly you're getting money, love, and a fancy new career sometime in the future?"

Liz laughed. "We think too much alike."

"Well, I suppose it's a possible angle, anyway. It's crazy to think someone could be killed over something like a psychic reading, though we have seen murders happen over a lot less," Morgan mused. "God, I don't even want to start thinking about a potential serial killer."

"Yeah, no. Me neither. Hold on a sec."

Morgan heard some muffled talking in the background.

"Hey, sorry, I'm going to have to go. Duty calls. But, real quick, I texted earlier because I found some notes from Ian's case. They were folded up and stuffed under a flap in the bottom of one of the banker's boxes holding another case's files. Not saying they were deliberately hidden, don't know yet, as the case numbers were similar. And I'm still vetting the information, but I feel like we're getting closer to finding out exactly who killed Ian. I am still keeping this all on the downlow on the outside chance the investigating detectives were trying to hide something."

Morgan took a deep breath and let it out. To bring her husband's killer to justice and put him away was one of the things that kept her going. It also kept her up most nights, replaying the details of the day he died. She needed justice for Ian, as much as she needed it for herself. Finding his killer might finally allow her to let go of the pain and grief she still carried inside and move on. An image of Caleb's face popped into her mind and she pushed it away. *Not that kind of moving on.* She sure as heck wasn't ready for that. "I can't thank you enough for all your help Liz," she said.

"Of course, Morgan. What are partners and friends for? You would do the same for me. I'll keep you posted. Miss you. Gotta go."

Morgan slipped the cellphone back in her pocket and leaned against the limestone wall of the Bijoux police station. Had the notes been misfiled or was there more to it? She couldn't think of anyone who would purposely muck up Ian's case. A veteran cop himself, Ian had been beloved by all. He'd mentored so many young detectives over the years. She knew there were bad eggs in the Detroit PD—heck, cops gossiped more than most people...but would one of them purposely hide or suppress crucial evidence in the murder of one of their own?

She sighed and carefully tucked away the churning emotions bubbling up. Ian's death still packed a wallop for her. The ache in her heart, the catch in the pit of her stomach. She rubbed her upper right arm, with its tattoo of the heart with a knife through it. Ian had had a matching tattoo. Five years. Five years since Ian was murdered. While the bone-jarring pain of losing him had lessened, it never really left. You don't forget the people you lose, they're always with you, just in a different way. At least she could now bear to remember the good times, along with the sorrow. She straightened and went back into the station.

"Did Liz have anything we could use?" JJ asked from behind his computer. He looked up when Morgan didn't answer right away. "You okay?"

"Yeah. Yeah, I'm fine." Morgan waved a hand. "She couldn't tell me much, other than it's an ongoing investigation. She did float an interesting theory, though. Maybe this person wants a better fortune. When they don't get it, they go off on the psychic. Weirder things have happened."

She could almost see the wheels turning in JJ's head as he considered the idea. His eyes took on a sharper look and his lips were pressed into a tight line. "I suppose it's possible. Maybe that's where the word 'Fraud' carved into the wax comes into play."

"Speaking of, have you heard back from Doc McVie about the autopsy results?"

"Did someone say Doc McVie? His ears must've been burning." JJ and Morgan turned toward the door as Maggie Cornet, Doc's assistant M.E. and former almost girlfriend of JJ, strode in carrying the box of evidence gathered from Edna's body. The tall, thin brunette placed the box on the front counter and smiled. "Hey, JJ."

JJ stood, retrieved the box, and headed toward the back room. "Thanks for bringing this by, Maggie," he said over his shoulder.

Maggie watched JJ walk away and smiled at Morgan. "He likes to play hard to get."

"You know JJ and Hannah are dating, right?"

"I've heard rumors, but these sorts of things are changeable, right?" She shrugged. "No sense in closing any doors just yet," she said and exited the station.

Morgan shook her head and checked her watch. It was almost time for the *Walk into The Light* orientation over at the Firefly Bed and Breakfast. "JJ, I'm going to head over to the Firefly and see if I can find any information on Edna," she called out. "See if Edna had any possible rivalries or enemies. Text me after you've gone through Doc's report and confirm cause of death."

"No need." He walked back out holding the folder. "Death by asphyxiation. She was strangled. Given the marks he found, likely with a rope."

"That's pretty damn personal," Morgan said. "You'd have to look a person straight in the eye while you killed them. It would take a fair amount of strength, too."

"Poor Edna." JJ shuddered. "Wood's trying to pull DNA from the neck markings, checking clothing, the usuals, but nothing yet."

Morgan's phone pinged. "Looks like Doctor Pete is almost done with Griselda. She'll be ready for pick up by end of day. I'll swing by there and get her as soon as I'm done at the B&B."

"You planning on keeping her here at the station?"

Morgan considered the question. This cat had no one and leaving it here alone, caged, seemed like cruel and unusual punishment. Especially after the trauma of losing her owner. "I'll keep her with me. No sense in upsetting the poor thing any more than she already has been."

"Ah, you do have a soft spot in there." JJ winked. When Morgan started to object, he raised his hand. "No worries. Your secret is safe with me."

CHAPTER 6

"WELCOME, psychics, tarot readers, empaths, intuitives, to our first annual *Walk into the Light Psychic Gathering.*" Caleb looked around the eight hundred square foot event room at the Firefly Bed and Breakfast. Not a full house but pretty close to it. He estimated about forty people had turned out for the opening night meet and greet. He was happy with the participation, especially considering it was the inaugural year. That and the fact that one of the psychics was now lying dead in the town morgue. *Or maybe that's what drew the crowd.* His eye caught Morgan's where she was standing at the back of the room. In a flash he remembered what it was like to have his arms around her. The night she saved his life. When he'd pulled her close and held on and she had fit perfectly against him. *Damn.*

Cal shook himself out of the memory and redirected his thoughts. Whatever the reason for the good turn-out, he hoped Morgan wouldn't scare anyone off with her official police business tone. She wasn't exactly open-minded when it came to the paranormal. "Hopefully, I didn't miss any of the categories."

"Palm Readers! Don't forget us. We always leave an imprint."

The crowd laughed.

Cal grinned. "Thank you for the reminder." He adjusted the microphone at the podium, raising it slightly to accommodate his six-foot frame. "I'm looking forward to spending time with each of you over the course of the long weekend. The psychic fair begins day after tomorrow, Saturday, ten a.m., at the Raven's Nest Bookstore. There will be another meet and greet at the bookstore tomorrow at noon, so you can see the table set up and your space. I hope you'll take advantage of the between times to visit our town shops and beach. If you've reserved a spot for the fair, you'll find a table with two chairs already set up for you. It'll have a tag with your name on it. I suggest you arrive around nine on Saturday if you're planning on personalizing your space. If you're bringing your own table and chairs, please arrive by eight a.m. so we can help you find a good spot to set up. The deck is all booked up, but we have available spots on the grass under the trees.

"Have you burned sage and energetically cleared the areas for us?" someone in the back asked. "After all, Bijoux *is* the most haunted town on the Lake Michigan coast. We can't have your spirits interfering with our personal spirit guides."

"Oh, and don't forget Messie," another person offered. "That Lake Michigan sea monster could show up anytime and disturb the energetic web."

"It's always hard to tell what Messie is going to do," Cal said. "But Rennie Buffet, owner of the Crystal Blue New Age Shop over in Lac Voo, will do the honors of calling in the directions and performing a sage cleansing before we start." He motioned to his right. "Rennie, would you please stand up so that everyone knows who you are?"

Rennie Buffet, a mid-sixties roundish woman with gray hair piled on top of her head and wearing a flowing black dress, stood and waved at the group. "Welcome to *Walk into the Light!*" she said. "For Saturday, I thought I'd do an overall clearing with sage, then go to each of your tables and clear you and your personal reading space as well."

"I'm allergic to sage," a psychic to the far left called out.

"Ah, I'll bring some Palo Santo and we'll do you and your area ahead of everyone else's," Rennie said. "Then you can go get a coffee while I finish the rest."

The psychic nodded and held her hands up in thanks.

"Of course, as one of you noted, this is a pretty darn haunted town so none of us, of course, can promise there won't be any shenanigans from the spirit world, no matter the precautions we take." She leaned toward the crowd. "We'll just have to be aware of where the messages are coming from when we read for our clients." She shrugged and smiled. "I'm sure you already do that anyway."

·⁺·⋆⁺ ☾ ⁺⋆·⁺·

MORGAN HAD BEEN HOVERING near the back of the event room, listening to the chatter coming from the audience and various people walking in and out, looking for anything out of the ordinary. Well, that was debatable here.

As Rennie was nearing the end of her Q and A session, Morgan strolled forward, her gaze scanning the colorful crowd. A few people were slumped in their seats, while others sat wide-eyed and seemed to be hanging on every word spoken by the woman who looked like an older version of Morgan's soon-to-be stepmom, Zoe. Morgan caught Cal's eye and motioned for him.

He nodded. "If you'll excuse me for just a moment, our fearless police captain, Morgan Hart, calls. Please go ahead and read through the agenda and I'll answer any questions in a few minutes."

Cal strode down the center aisle and followed Morgan as she stepped outside the room. "What's up that couldn't wait? I'm in the middle of orientation."

"Nice to see you, too."

"I know you well enough to know this isn't a social call. Do you have news about Edna?"

Morgan sighed. "Yes. Confirmation she was murdered. Strangled. Doc is still searching for any DNA that's not hers or anything else that can help us." She leaned in toward him, catching just the faintest scent of pine, and whispered, "There have been two other murders, similar to our victim's, in the past three months. Traverse City and Detroit."

Cal's eyebrows shot up. "Well, that doesn't bode well, does it?"

"No, it does not." Morgan's chin pointed in the direction of the audience. "What do you really know about this group? Any rivalries I should know about?"

"Not that I'm aware of." He paused for a moment, then grabbed her hand and pulled her toward the stage. "Let's find out."

What the hell? Morgan yanked her hand free. "Stop being so dramatic," she stage-whispered "And we've already discussed this. I don't want you investigating."

"Not investigating. Just helping."

She stopped mid aisle, forcing him to stop too. Cal turned to her. "What's this really about?"

Morgan looked away, not meeting his eyes, but noting every other eye in the room was on both of them. "I can't keep you safe if you insist on inserting yourself into the middle of things," she said in a real whisper. "Look what almost happened last time."

"Ah. Okay. Here on out, I absolve you from any responsibility." He resumed walking her to the stage and pulled her up to the dais.

"You know it doesn't work like that."

Cal's eyes met hers. "It does this time." He pulled the mike from its stand. "I'm so very sorry to have to share this news with you, but Captain Hart has just confirmed it was, indeed, our dear friend, Madame Edna Marisol, who was dead found yesterday at Lac Voo Nature Preserve."

"It was murder!" a deep male voice boomed from the back of the room.

A wave of gasps and exclamations rippled through the audience.

Morgan grabbed the microphone from Cal. "The gentleman who shouted out 'It was Murder.' Can you please stand and share with us why you think it's murder? Do you have information or details?" She glanced around the room, her eyes landing on an imposing man who stood and crossed his arms over his chest. He was about six foot three, two hundred-forty pounds, silver gray hair, full-on Tom Selleck *Magnum* mustache. "And you are...?"

"Jack Steve, at your service." He bowed and the crowd applauded.

"He's our guest speaker this weekend," Cal whispered to Morgan.

She nodded and whispered back to Cal, "Yeah, I recognize the two first names." Morgan waved Jack up to the stage. He walked up to Morgan and nodded at Cal. Morgan cupped her hand over the mic and addressed the older man. "Did you know Edna?"

"Of course," he said, his feet braced apart. "Most everyone here knew Edna." He turned toward the gathered attendees and said in a booming voice, "Edna was one of us. She was our dear, dear friend and taken much too soon."

The psychics applauded. A few whistled or cheered. Rocky Banks — Edna's now former protégé—sobbed, while Davey Rocket leaned back in his chair and rearranged his ponytail, and Daisy shot Jack a glare that could freeze Lake Michigan in August. Morgan duly catalogued the notable reactions. She'd ponder them later. Turning back to Jack she asked, "And why would you say she was murdered? Did you know of anyone who had a problem with Madame Marisol?"

"I said what I did because of a premonition, of course." He addressed both Morgan and the gathering, his expression solemn. "Edna came to me in a dream and I knew at that very moment she was gone from this plane of existence."

"Your evidence is a dream?" Morgan suppressed an eye roll and simply shook her head. "I don't mean to disparage your beliefs — or whatever you call them — but I'm looking for *real* information."

"Oh, his premonitions are always real," Rocky offered from his seat in the front row. He wiped at his eyes with a hanky, leaving a streak of black mascara across each cheek. "Edna always trusted whatever Mr. Steve had to say." He smiled up at the older man and Jack went over to him and patted his shoulder.

"Poppycock!"

Everyone looked toward the back of the room where a man had just entered. Morgan took in his appearance. Late sixty-something, medium height, buzzed silver hair, goatee, a tee shirt emblazoned with 'Power to the People' and a protest fist, jeans, black Chucks. "And who would you be, Mr. Poppycock?" *Who even says poppycock anymore?*

Rennie ran over to the man and hugged him. They walked up to the podium, arm in arm. When he reached Morgan, he extended a hand. "Starman McGee." He shot Jack Steve a look that told Morgan there was no love lost there. "Also, at your service."

Jack harrumphed and crossed his arms over his chest again.

"I'm guessing Starman isn't your real name?" Morgan asked.

"Not from birth, but I had it legally changed in the '80s."

"Starman is my...paramour," Rennie offered with a slight blush. "He's here to help me with the pop-up shop I'm setting up over at Cal's place for the psychic fair."

Rennie leaned into Starman's chest and wrapped her arms around him. Starman gave her a squeeze in return as he threw a frown at Jack over the top of her head.

"What's going on here?" Morgan asked.

"I'm hugging my man," Rennie said.

"Not that." Her chin pointed back and forth between the two men. "You two don't like each other." She looked at Starman. "And you didn't like Edna, based on your 'poppycock' comment. So, I ask again, what's going on here?"

Jack laughed a little. "Just a friendly rivalry amongst psychics. Nothing more."

"And nothing you need to worry about," Starman added. "Jack here is just an old windbag. As was Edna. Two peas in that old-timey pod, so it's no surprise he's defending her. Plus, she always gave him free readings." Starman rolled his eyes. "Dude lives for free readings."

Morgan held up a hand. "I get it. No love lost." *And we'll continue this conversation later in private, down at the station.* For the moment, she'd wait to see if any other tidbits popped up.

"None whatsoever," Jack said with a frown of his own. He turned to Morgan. "Look, I've worked with the L.A. police force for many years. I offer you my investigative services to help solve this egregious crime."

"Thank you, but no." Aside from the mustache, Jack looked like an older version of Caleb; good looking and irritating and likely to completely ignore anything she said.

Cal motioned the universal 'call me' hand signal to Jack. Morgan gave him a sharp glance. Cal shrugged. Morgan shook her head and turned to address the entire gathering.

"Please let me know if anyone sees or hears anything unusual. Or if you have any information about Edna Marisol which may help further the investigation. Cal has my contact info, or you can reach me at the police station in town."

"Do you mean unusual like the 19th century pirate ghost standing behind you?" Daisy offered. She shook her head. "No, no, I suppose that's not all that odd, given the history of this town."

The crowd murmured their agreement.

"By the way, Morgan dear, it's nice to meet you. Zoe has told me so much about the wonderful job you're doing here in Bijoux," Rennie said with a warm smile. "Also, there's an older woman next to the pirate who looks a lot like you. Your mother, perhaps? I think she wants to tell you something."

Morgan stiffened. Pirates were one thing, the possibility of her mom hanging out behind her was another. It was all she could do *not* to look over her shoulder. Even though she knew Billie was always with her on some level, there was *still* no such thing as ghosts. Not even a chance of them existing, she reminded herself as the *Ghostbusters* theme song rang through her head. She handed the microphone back to Cal. "On that note, they're all yours." She turned to leave, then stopped and said over her shoulder, "Oh, and I'm on my way to pick up the cat, so you're officially off cat duty."

"Huh." Cal looked dejected.

Morgan pursed her lips. "Fine, you can have visitation rights."

He perked back up. "Excellent. I have some special treats for her."

Before Morgan could respond, Rocky said, "Griselda knew all of Madame's secrets. If anyone knows what happened, it'll be that cat." He pulled his shawl tight around his shoulders and frowned. "Griselda and I never really saw eye to eye on most things, but I can keep her if you want. I'm probably the closest to family she has."

"I might be able to communicate with her," Daisy offered. "I'm also a pet psychic. Cats are my specialty. I'll come by and see her tomorrow, determine if she's hiding anything. Cats can be that way, you know. Very private and secretive."

Morgan stared at Daisy and Rocky. He acted like the cat was his sister or something and she seemed to think Griselda would talk to her. *I'm done here.* "Thanks, but we're good. I'm keeping Griselda in custody until the case is solved." She turned to the small crowd. "Again, if any of you think of anything, please reach out to me or my deputy, JJ. And please also know we're doing everything we can to assure a safe and productive weekend for all of you."

CHAPTER 7

MORGAN SLID into the driver's seat of her truck in the parking lot of the Firefly, her stomach growled. Loudly. She checked her smart watch. How was it 5:30 already? All she'd eaten today was that muffin for breakfast, didn't even get to enjoy the decadence of Zoe's cinnamon butter coffee cake. While investigating a murder was the priority, she reminded herself she had to do better about keeping herself fed and her energy up. She patted her stomach. "Fine, fine. I'll feed you, but we have to get Griselda first." Morgan pulled away from the sunset pink B&B and headed toward Doctor Pete's Veterinary Clinic.

Twenty minutes later, Morgan parked along Main Street, just across from the vet office. It was housed in one of the old board and batten buildings sitting on the edge of Progress. 'Progress' is what the locals disparagingly called the gentrified area. Doc Pete was one of the Hold Outs the mayor had recently begun criticizing during one of his stump speeches.

Morgan pulled open the heavy oak and glass door to the vet clinic and a bell chimed overhead. "Be right with you," a male voice called out. The doc, late thirties, blond hair, short stocky build, walked out of one of the two exam rooms, wiping his hands on a paper towel. "Oh, hi Captain. How are you this evening?"

"I'm good." Her stomach growled loudly. "Well, apparently I'll be better after I get some food in me. Do you have Griselda ready to go?"

"I certainly do." He disappeared to the back and returned with the large cat in her carrier, placing it gently on the front desk. "This one here is in excellent health. She doesn't seem to be carrying any long-term trauma from the attack on her owner." He shrugged. "But it is a cat, so who can tell. They're not like dogs, who wear their hearts on their furry little sleeves."

Morgan peered into the cage. Griselda stared back with her large gold eyes. "What a beauty you are," she whispered. She straightened. "Did you find anything out of the ordinary? From the state of van, we've concluded there was a struggle. I wondered if she may have picked up something during the commission of the crime."

"Actually, yes. There was blood on her nails. I took scrapings and sent them off for DNA testing. Then my assistant cleaned her up and gave her a good brushing. We'll go through the fur collected to see if there's anything out of the ordinary." He scratched the cat's nose through the cage grate. "I'll let you know if we find something. Also, when the DNA results come in."

"Perfect. What do I owe you?"

He waved a hand. "Oh, nothing. I don't mind supporting our police." He took a breath. "Although, I wouldn't mind grabbing a cup of coffee sometime...?"

"Coffee?"

"Would beer be better?" he quickly added.

"I'm sorry. Are you asking me out?"

Doc Pete froze. Before he could answer, Griselda batted at Morgan's hand through the cage and howled. "I'd better get her some food, too. Thanks for helping us out." She gathered up the cage and opened the front door. "And please let me or JJ know as soon as you get the results in."

"Will do," Doc called after her. "And let me know about coffee. Or beer," he said, but Morgan was already out the door.

MORGAN CARRIED Griselda down the street and into The Perch Mouth Bar and Grille. Not much to look at, with its narrow shotgun design and rustic — read: worn — exterior, but it was the local dive and she loved it. Plus, her oldest friend in the world now owned it. She sat down at the old oak bar with its aged and faded yellow linoleum counter. People had autographed it over the years with Sharpies of every color.

"Hey, sweet thing." Her friend, bartender, and bar owner, Francine

'Frankie' Whitaker hugged her across the bar then pulled a draft of Motor City Mustang Stout and placed it in front of Morgan. Frankie nodded toward the cat. "A bowl of water for your friend there?"

"Water and cat chow, please. I know you have some, with that clowder you feed in the alley. I'm going to park her behind the bar, though, okay?" Morgan smiled. "I don't want to upset any of your customers, but I also didn't want to leave her in the truck."

"Sure. Over there is fine." Frankie motioned to an empty corner. "Tell me how things are going, how you're doing. Connie's been all over the news with her claims of another Detroit Killer in our midst."

"Of course, she has. And of course, there's no Detroit Killer." Morgan inhaled deeply and sighed at the scent of rich coffee, chocolate, and hops. She took a long drink. *Almost as good as food.* "There's absolutely no 'Detroit Killer.' It's true, though, there was another murder out at the Preserve. I'm also working through some other news dropped on me today: Dad and Zoe are getting married this weekend. Well, on Monday."

"What?!? When did this happen? Scoop me!"

"They just told me this morning. Apparently decided to go through with it while so many of Zoe's psychic friends are in town."

Frankie opened a bottled beer and handed it to a customer a couple of seats down, then put a bowl of water and cat food in Griselda's cage and reclosed it. "And how are you feeling about this?"

Morgan sighed. "Honestly, it's a little challenging. Even though Dad and Mom were divorced for such a long time, it's still weird to think of him married to someone else." She took a sip of her beer. "But that's my issue, not theirs, and I'm happy for Zoe and Dad." She smiled. "We have to find happiness when and where we can, right?"

Frankie patted Morgan's hand and gave it a squeeze. "Of course, you're happy for them. And you'd do well to take your own advice."

"Maybe someday." Morgan scrunched up her face. "Once I solve the mystery of Ian's murder, maybe then I'll be able to start over."

"Is this seat taken?"

Morgan glanced over at the guy who was asking. Medium height, medium build, medium thirties, medium coloring, lots of mediums, lots of khaki. Like he bought his clothes at an adult Garanimal store. "Nope, help yourself."

He pulled the stool up to the counter and ordered one of the local IPAs before turning to Morgan. "Trent."

She didn't look at him. "And?"

"Trent. It's my name."

She raised her glass. "Nice to meet you. Are you a psychic? If so, please keep any predictions to yourself. I'm done today."

He laughed. "No, no. I'm not psychic." He paused. "Not that I can tell, anyway. How does one even know if they're psychic? Or have powers of any kind?"

Morgan glanced over at him again. There was absolutely nothing powerful emanating from him. "Maybe you should be asking one of the many psychics in town for the weekend.

"Maybe." He angled his head toward her. "Honestly, though, I think it's a bunch of bunk. But my dad believed in them so I thought it might be interesting to check it out as long as I'm here, visiting Bijoux."

Bunk. She could accept that. Morgan turned back to her beer. "Okay, then."

"You're not very chatty, are you," Trent said.

"You got that right," Frankie offered with a chuckle as she placed a plate of fish and chips with homemade coleslaw in front of Morgan.

"Frankie here is the real psychic." Morgan quirked a smile at her friend. "She knew what I wanted without even telling her."

Trent considered the bartender. Frankie held up her hands. "Nope, not psychic. Just twenty five years of friendship." She laughed. "And that cop brain of hers is always ticking away, even when she's quiet."

"Cop? You don't look like a cop."

Not the first time she'd heard that. People always underestimated her on that front. She didn't mind so much, though. Sometimes it worked to her advantage. "I'm going to assume you meant that in a good way."

"The town's best captain," Cal said as he dropped into the seat on the other side of Morgan.

"Only captain," Morgan said. *And why is everyone crowding around me?*

"Which makes you the best." Cal jostled her shoulder with his.

Morgan's stomach fluttered at the unexpected touch. *Traitor*.

Frankie shook her head and filled a glass of Traverse City Cherry Hard Cider for him. "You are walking into dangerous territory tonight, my friend."

"Always am." He toasted Frankie and took a sip. "Keeps life interesting." Cal turned to the guy on the other side of Morgan. "Catching a vacation before the season ends?" he asked.

"Yeah, something like that."

Rocky walked in the door and sat on the stool next to Trent. "Hi Captain, Caleb," he said with a little wave.

Morgan looked over. There was a definite shift in the air around Edna's old protégé. "You seem happier than the last time I saw you."

Rocky grinned. "Honestly, I feel happier. Lighter. I've decided to step into full-on psychic reader this weekend and wear the title proudly. No more apprenticing, no more giant cat bossing me around. I'm free." He looked at Frankie. "I'll have whatever Cal's having. It looks delicious. A grilled cheese, too, please. Extra pickles."

"What was holding you back?" Trent asked.

"The Mystical Madame Edna Marisol. She was mentoring me, but she's gone now. After two years of kowtowing in servitude to her, it's my time to shine and share my abilities with the world." Rocky glanced at Morgan. "Not that I don't miss her. Edna will always have a special place in my heart. She was like a grumpy grandmother to me."

Morgan nodded as she added Rocky to the very short list of suspects she'd been mentally tabulating. Actually, she had no suspects on her radar, but Rocky just made a spectacular appearance.

"Tell me, how unhappy were you, exactly?" Morgan leaned on the counter and looked past Trent.

"Oh, I don't mean to sound ungrateful. Or calloused, for that matter. I felt ready to spread my energetic wings for a while now, but Edna kept telling me I wasn't ready." Rocky took a sip of his hard cider. He turned and looked Morgan directly in the eye. "I tell you, I *was* ready."

"I'm a big fan of your look." Everyone at the bar turned toward the man who dropped into the seat on the other side of Rocky. Morgan took in his stats: mid-late twenties; longish red hair, thick build. "You're one of the psychics, aren't you?" He extended his hand to Rocky. "I'm Jimmy. Jimmy Canard."

Rocky smiled. "Nice to meet you, Jimmy Canard. Yes, I am one of the psychics." He shook the other man's hand. "And thank you. It's taken me years to get to a place where I'm happy with my professional appearance." He looked around at everyone at the bar. "What? It's not like there's a handbook telling you how to dress, you know."

"Are there handbooks for other things?" Trent asked.

Rocky seemed to consider the question, then replied, "No, I suppose not. It's why us young mystical-types try to get someone with experience to mentor us."

"So, back to your mentor," Morgan said. "Talk some more about how dissatisfied you were with Edna's coaching."

"This seems more like an interrogation than a conversation. Nice to meet all of you, but I'm outta here," Trent said. He dropped a ten on the bar and headed out the door.

Morgan gave Trent a slight wave and continued to stare at Rocky. Rocky stared back.

Frankie brought the grilled cheese. Rocky picked up his plate and cider and stood. "If you don't mind, I'm going to sit elsewhere. I'm really too exhausted to talk about this right now. I need to get my head on so I'm ready to take my place at the psychic fair when it opens."

"Mind if I join you?" Dave asked. "I always enjoy hearing stories from real psychics."

"Sure, why not? I haven't been doing this long, but I do have some juicy gossip," Rocky answered and the pair moved to an open table in the corner of the bar.

Morgan watched Rocky for a moment, then turned back to the bar and her food. There'd be time tomorrow for more questions, but she needed to get organized in her mind first. Maybe take another look at the purple wizard van, see if she and JJ missed anything that could point directly to Rocky's potential involvement.

"Huh. Guess those three didn't think we were good company," Cal said.

"You're not," Morgan said as she squirted ketchup onto her plate.

"He left because Morgan's such a cop sometimes." Frankie winked at Morgan. "He was getting ready to start hitting on our friend before you, that psychic showed up." Frankie paused. "Do psychics have groupies? Because I'm pretty sure that's what Jimmy is."

"No idea. And for heaven's sake. Why would you say that guy was going to ask me out? That's not at all what happened."

Frankie pointed at her head. "Bartender's intuition. I see it all the time."

"Yeah, I don't think so. But Doc Pete is another story. He *did* ask me out. At least I think he did." She rubbed her forehead. "It's been so long since I had a date, literally a decade I'm not sure I can recognize the signs anymore."

Frankie and Cal leaned toward Morgan at the same time. "Details." Frankie demanded.

"What exactly did he say?" Cal asked. He leaned even closer.

Morgan instinctively moved slightly away from Cal. She was used to being the interrogator, not the interrogatee. There was an intensity in Cal's tone that told her the tables had definitely shifted. She met his gaze, and it took a couple of heartbeats before she could look away. Her stomach flipped again. *Damn him.* "Just something like, want to grab a coffee or beer sometime?"

"Sounds date-like," Frankie said. "So, what was your answer?"

"I asked him if he was asking me out. Then Gris let out a bloodcurdling howl and the tone of the conversation changed." Morgan shrugged. "How weird is that?"

"I'll tell you what's weird," Cal said in a blunt tone. "You asking Doc Pete if he was asking you out." He shook his head.

Morgan squared her shoulders. "And why is that weird?"

"Don't take offense." He sighed. "Look, you're one of the smartest humans I know. You miss absolutely nothing when you're in cop mode. Drop into normal person mode, though, and it's like you don't know how to function." He leaned back in his chair and took a drink. "I'm not criticizing, mind you. Just an observation. I sometimes even like that side of you." He smiled.

"Wow," Frankie said. "You hit the nail on the head Cal. Although I would add that she's a bit better now than when we were kids. But only a bit." Frankie smiled at her friend. "I think she was born to be a cop."

Morgan huffed. "If you're both done analyzing me, I'd like to eat my food in peace."

"And how often does that actually happen?" Cal asked as he grabbed a fry off her plate and took a bite. "Needs salt."

"If you even think about salting my food for me, I *will* break your arm"

"Cal, don't push it," Frankie said. She exchanged a glance with Morgan. Long years of friendship meant Morgan didn't need to say anything. Her eyes said it all. "Enough with the teasing, Morgan has a lot on her mind."

Cal cleared his throat and had the decency to look sheepish. He picked up his hard cider and took a long drink.

Morgan gave Frankie a grateful smile. At least she could now eat her dinner in relative quiet. But that didn't erase the fact she was dealing with another murderer in Bijoux. And it also didn't erase the fact she'd been asked out on a date. For some reason the date thing was bothering her more at the moment. Maybe it was because it shook loose the cobwebs of the past and the fact she still hadn't solved Ian's murder. And she just couldn't allow herself to move on until she did.

CHAPTER 8

MORGAN LEFT the Perch Mouth around ten p.m. and headed for the lakeside cottage she'd inherited from her mom. Billie had loved this place and Morgan did too. It was starting to feel like home, now that she'd started painting and doing repairs. She was grateful her dad had taught her how to fix things; it meant she didn't have to rely on anyone else. And the colors she used were 'just right' — traditional beachy tones of blue-green, soft white, with a pop of orange, inside and out.

"I have just the spot for you when we get there," Morgan said to Griselda. "My place isn't big, but we'll put your litterbox in the laundry room and your carrier in my bedroom. That way, you have a little hideaway if you feel the need to be alone."

Griselda mewed.

"Exactly. I, too, understand the importance of personal space. Unlike most of the humans around me." She frowned, then smiled. She was well aware she wore her gruffness like an armor. If she were going to be completely honest with herself, it was good to have friends and family who could see past it and love her anyway.

Morgan pulled the truck up to the cottage, shut it off, and took the cat inside. Once loose, Gris ran a few laps through each of the rooms, then settled into Morgan's favorite spot on the worn, brown leather sofa. "Hey, that's where I sit."

Gris responded by licking her tail and immediately falling asleep. Morgan checked her watch. Ten thirty. "Okay. You can sleep there for now, but only because I'm heading for bed myself."

The cat opened one eye in response, sighed, and turned her head.

Morgan rolled the tension out of her shoulders and headed for her bedroom. "Cats."

MORGAN STOOD outside the front door of the police station at eight a.m. the next morning, debating how to get it open without dropping the cat carrier or litter box. She decided to give it a little kick. JJ jumped up from his desk, pushed the door open, and held it for Morgan. "That's a lot of cat. And cat stuff."

"There's more in the back of the truck. Would you please get it?" Morgan asked as she made her way through the station, hands still full. "I'm going to park the litter box and crate in the cell."

"Makes sense. It's not like it really gets used all that much." JJ retrieved the container of litter, food, and dishes and placed it on the cell cot.

"Did you close the front door? I want to let Gris out so she can stretch those long legs of hers."

"Closed up tight." JJ emptied the litter into the box and set it in the corner. He then proceeded to fill the bowls with dry food and water.

"Hey, you're good at this."

"Little Dog has trained me well." Little Dog was JJ's Chihuahua, confidante, and best friend. Aside from his girlfriend, Hannah, that is.

Morgan opened the crate door and Griselda took a tentative step out. After being free to roam Morgan's cottage last night, she wasn't all that happy about being crated again. The cat stretched a single back leg, then bolted out of the cell. "Hey!" Morgan yelled.

JJ shook his head. "It's what cats do." He pushed the crate under the cot. "Where did you get all this stuff? I don't recall seeing any of it beyond the chow and crate in Edna's van."

"Doc Pete. He gifted it all to me when I picked Gris up last night. Said something about wanting to help the police out." Morgan shrugged. "It's not like we have extra in the budget for cat things, so I accepted. He also found some blood on her claws and sent it in for DNA testing. Maybe we'll get a lead."

"Ah, the *vet*."

"Why did you say it like that?"

"I hear he's sweet on you."

Morgan stopped arranging the cat stuff and turned to her deputy.

"Where did you hear that?" Her eyes narrowed. "Who have you been talking to?"

JJ held up his hands in surrender. "I saw Cal at Dave's when I was grabbing coffee this morning. He may have mentioned it."

Damn him. The man was always sticking his nose in where it did not belong. She crossed her arms and stared at JJ. "What else did he say?"

JJ stared back. "Great news on the claw blood. For the rest, I plead the fifth," he said and exited the cell. "Hey kitty, kitty. Where'd you go?"

Morgan stomped to her desk and started to drop into her seat when she realized the cat had taken it over. And was snuggling Bubbles, one of her Powerpuff Girl figures. "Oh, no, we're not going to play with those, Miss Gris," she said as she carefully extracted it from the large paws. Morgan scratched behind Griselda's ears. "And I need my seat, so go find somewhere else to sleep. If you recall, we're working to find out who killed your person."

Griselda let out a soft mew and Morgan thought her heart was going to melt. She was definitely getting a cat after this case was solved. She considered the Maine Coon. *Maybe, when this case is closed and if it's all right with you, I'll be your new person.*

"So how'd it go with the mayor yesterday?" JJ asked.

Morgan grimaced as she booted up her desktop. "As well as can be expected. I'll be happy when the election is over since it seems to be where he puts his priorities. He actually criticized us for not running enough patrols." She threw JJ a glance over her shoulder. "Hey, didn't you tell me once we had a group of volunteer deputies?"

"Yeah, your dad started the program one summer during the Fourth of July parade. The town was split over the march route and arguments were heating up between the groups. Able brought in some volunteers to help keep the peace." He looked over at Morgan. "That was the first and last time we used them, though."

"Well, we only need them to drive around at night, nothing else. Just a reassuring police presence."

"Okay, I'll make some calls. Should I reach out to Arnie, too?" Arnie Hart was Morgan's uncle and the county sheriff.

"Let's see how we do with the deputies first, though I appreciate the thought." She smiled. "You're the best, JJ."

JJ grinned. "Yes ma'am."

The station door opened and in walked Rennie, Davey Rocket, Daisy of the one first name, and Jack Steve of the two first names. "Can we help you?" JJ asked.

"*We* are here to help *you*," Jack replied and deposited a box of Hannah's pastries and two coffees on the counter.

Morgan approached the front counter and peered in the box. Bear claws. Her mouth watered, but she would not be bought so easily. She closed the box and crossed her arms over her chest. "Thank you for the coffee and donuts, but I thought I was pretty clear yesterday. None of you were to get involved."

"The L.A. police were a little hesitant at first to accept my help back in the '80s. Until I started leading them to bodies, that is." Jack said.

Morgan's eyes narrowed. "And exactly how did you know where the bodies were?" she asked, wondering now if anyone had ever looked into Jack Steve's background. She assumed the L.A. police did before hiring him, but she'd have to verify. Criminals were known to sometimes insert themselves into investigations. She made a mental note to do some research into the man.

"It's the cat." Daisy interrupted, looking off into the distance. "She spoke to me last night."

The officers looked at each other, skepticism ran unspoken between them, then back at Daisy. Davey poked at her arm. "Go on, tell them what the beast told you."

"So, as I mentioned yesterday, besides being a regular-type psychic, I'm also a pet-type psychic. Sometimes animals tell me things. Griselda came to me in a dream." She shivered. "She said Edna was strangled." Daisy shook her head. "Poor thing saw it all. She tried to help Edna, but the killer was just too strong for her."

Morgan leaned forward. The confirmation that Edna had been murdered by strangulation hadn't been released yet, only that a death had occurred. The blood on Griselda's claws might confirm she had, indeed, tried to protect Edna. While she didn't believe this woman could talk to animals, Daisy may have witnessed something and not realized it. Morgan had seen it before. The subconscious acting out. Or, maybe she knew more than she was letting on. "Anything else?"

"That was all. I'd like a moment with the cat if that's okay. If I touch her, maybe I can get more details." She glanced around the station. "We stopped at the vet's office first and he said Griselda was probably here."

JJ motioned to Morgan's desk. "She's in the captain's chair over there."

Daisy walked up to Gris and crouched down, so she was looking eye to eye with the feline. Gris growled, low and deep. A cat warning if Morgan had ever heard one. "I'm not sure she wants you to bother her right now," Morgan called out.

"Nonsense. *All* animals love me," Daisy said with a smile. She reached out to pet the cat and in the span of a heartbeat, Gris was up on all fours, fur on end, and hissing at the older woman.

"Well, apparently you found one who doesn't," Morgan said.

Daisy shook her head. "She's so angry, there's no way to get any information out of her right now." She stood and straightened her patchwork maxi dress. "I'm positive it has nothing to do with me, though."

"Sure," Morgan muttered. She turned to the other psychics. "Was there anything else? Aren't you supposed to be over at the bookstore to look at the set up?"

Davey checked his phone for the time. "We've reserved a spot, but I suppose we should get moving along. Daisy?"

"The only image I'm getting is wax and tarot cards. Though she's also wondering where Rocky is." Daisy looked at Morgan. "They had a horrible sibling rivalry and Griselda is relieved to not be around him right now, so she can mourn in peace." She continued to watch the cat. "Edna wasn't always nice. I just know there's more Griselda wants to tell me." She sighed and walked back to her husband.

"What do you mean?" Morgan asked, recalling the way Daisy had glared yesterday at the orientation when Jack said what a kind woman Edna was. "Did you two have an issue?"

Daisy laughed and Morgan thought it sounded more than a little nervous. "What aren't you telling me, Daisy?"

Davey stepped forward. "No interrogation without legal representation."

Morgan crossed her arms. "I'm not interrogating. I'm simply asking questions based on her own words."

Daisy placed a hand on Davey's arm. "It's okay." She squared her shoulders and held her arms out. "Go ahead. Arrest me. Pop those cuffs on."

"For what?!?" Morgan asked. "What are talking about?"

"For whatever made up charge you have in mind to take me down." Daisy looked Morgan up and down. "You and Edna. Just the same. Accusing when there's no evidence of anything."

"What did Edna accuse you of?"

"Making her coffee taste bad. People hated it, so came back to us. She made horrible coffee. And we *are* the host family, so they should've come to us first, anyway."

Morgan had heard enough. She walked around the desk and opened the front door. "Thank you so much for the information. Have a good day." Daisy and Davey exited, but Jack and Rennie stayed. "Was there something else?"

"We're going with you to see Zoe," Rennie said.

"I didn't say I was going over there."

Rennie just looked at her with a knowing smile. *Damn.* Well, she could've easily assumed Morgan might need to check in about details for the upcoming wedding. *No such thing as psychics,* Morgan reminded herself.

"Fine. Give me a sec." She walked back to JJ, leaned over and whispered, "Run a background on both Jack Steve and Starman McGee."

JJ glanced over at one of the subjects in question, then back at Morgan. "Yeah, I get that."

Morgan straightened. "Back in a bit, JJ. I'm going to run by the Raven's Nest, then you and I will head out to the Preserve and see if we missed anything. Please follow up on the case items we discussed."

JJ saluted. "Yes, ma'am. You know I'm on it." Griselda howled and everyone turned toward Morgan's desk. The cat was sitting up in her chair as if she'd start using the computer at any minute. "I'll remind her where her food is, first."

THE TRIO WALKED out into the cool morning air. Main Street was buzzing with a fair number of colorful folks, all with coffee or tea in hand, many heading towards the Raven's Nest bookstore. *A zombie march if there ever was one*, Morgan thought, then forced the image out of her mind. She had to remain impartial if she was going to do her job properly.

"Did you two just meet this weekend?" Morgan asked Rennie and Jack as they made their way across the street to Hal's.

"Oh, heavens no," Rennie said. "I've known Jack forever." She patted his arm and he smiled. "He and Zoe were engaged in the early eighties, before she moved back east."

Morgan stopped in the center of the street. "Excuse me?"

Jack chuckled and nodded. "Ah, yes. Those were the days. Just two psychics embarking on an amazing adventure of love and the afterlife in L.A."

Suddenly feeling protective, Morgan asked, "Does my dad know about this?"

"I'm sure I don't know, but I can't imagine Zoe would keep something like this from him," Rennie said. "We believe in honesty."

A car pulled up and stopped. The driver hung his head out the window. "If you don't mind...?"

Morgan waved. "Sorry." They finished crossing the street and walked into Hal's.

"I know that's you, Rennie. I can sense you anywhere!" Zoe called from the coffee bar at the back of the store.

Rennie laughed. "And I come bearing gifts."

Zoe met them halfway and stopped. "Oh, my goddess. Jack? Is that really you?"

Jack walked up and embraced Zoe in a bear hug, almost lifting her off the ground with the force of it. "I'm here," was all he said.

Zoe leaned back, looked into his eyes, and smiled. "You certainly are."

"What's all the ruckus about?" Able asked as he walked out of the back of the store. "And what's *this* all about?" he asked Zoe, who was standing with her arms still around Jack.

Zoe pivoted to face him. "Able, this is Jack Steve. I told you all about him."

"I was her first real love," Jack said, in that proud-alpha-male-do not challenge me-way.

Able squinted at the other man. Morgan knew that look and nothing good ever came of it. "So, Dad, how about a cup of that famous coffee of yours?"

"I'd love one too," Rennie added. "Nice to see you, Able." She gave him a hug, artfully turning him back toward the coffee bar. "Zoe tells me you have some new paint samples in. I'm thinking of repainting the Blue Crystal and would love to take a look."

Able harrumphed but allowed himself to be led away. "Don't think I don't know when I'm being manipulated. I was a cop for a lot of years, you know."

Morgan patted his shoulder. "No worries Dad." She leaned and whispered in his ear while she walked with them. "Remember, she's marrying *you*. In three days." She felt him relax and smiled. "Speaking of, I wanted to check in with you and Zoe. What can I do to help with the wedding?"

"Don't worry about, Morgan. You have your hands full right now."

"Dad, we've had this conversation. I'm here and I want to help."

Able nodded, smiling. "Okay, we'll let you know."

Jack and Zoe walked up to the coffee counter. "Rennie, we should probably head over to the set-up," Jack said.

Rennie nodded. "Want to come along, Zoe? Starman is there. We're putting together our shop booth."

"I'd love to see him!" She looked over at Able. "You good with things if I leave for a bit?"

"I'm good." Able kissed her cheek. "Have fun with your friends."

As the trio headed to the front door, Morgan walked up behind them. "I was planning on checking things out. I'll walk over with you."

Zoe smiled and linked her arm with Morgan's, then she froze. Morgan glanced first at Zoe then back at her dad who was watching carefully.

Rennie turned to her sister. "What do you see, Sis?"

"A crystal with writing on it. So much darkness." Her eyes focused on Morgan. "Let it go, Fay. You're putting yourself in danger."

Morgan blanched. Fay was her middle name and Ian was the only one who ever called her that. She might not believe in psychics, but this was creepy. And not the first time Zoe had supposedly given her a message from Ian.

Zoe shook her head as if to clear it. "Nothing. Nothing else."

Jack rubbed her back. "Just like the good old days."

Able cleared his throat and Jack dropped his hand.

"Let's go," Morgan said. "Because obviously what I need right now is to surround myself with *more* psychics."

CHAPTER 9

ZOE AND JACK walked around the back of the Raven's Nest and entered the psychic fair set up through a wrought iron gate while Morgan hung back and observed the activity. She loved the bookstore and was honestly happy to see it as a vibrant hub of activity in her community. Never mind this particular activity, a psychic fair, was a little much. The old board and batten building had been a second home for her as a child and Cal's great uncle Baptiste treated her like one of his own. Well, in his own gruff way. Morgan smiled, then shook off the trip down memory lane. She had a murder to solve.

"So, Captain Hart, what new information do you have for our viewers?"

Morgan spun around to find Connie holding a mike in her face. She frowned. "Nothing new, Connie."

"Nothing new? Or is it that you have nothing you're willing to share with our good townsfolk? I can only imagine the worry and concern everyone is feeling right now." She looked directly into the camera. "I know I'm certainly feeling it. I find myself constantly looking over my shoulder for the Detroit Killer."

"What you're actually feeling is you'd like to boost your ratings by concocting stories where there are none." Morgan turned to leave and Connie grabbed her arm. Morgan stared at it until the other woman released her and stepped back.

Connie turned the mike off and told the camerawoman to go get some mood shots of the psychics setting up. "How is Woodsy? I know you talked to him yesterday at the crime scene."

"You should ask him yourself."

"I'm trying to honor our break, but it's hard." She glanced at Morgan, frowning. "I miss him."

Morgan sighed. "I'm sorry you're having troubles. Give him a few more days. Maybe he'll be willing to talk then."

Connie brightened. "Do you think so?"

"Doc's never been one to hold a grudge." The sounds of an argument from the back of the bookstore caught Morgan's attention. "I need to go. Good luck."

Morgan rounded the side of the building and entered the gate. Rennie, Jack, and Starman – what was his real name, anyway? – were all talking loudly around a pop-up tent. "You absolutely cannot set your tent up here, Rennie," Jack said. "You're practically on top of a ley line, for heaven's sake." He huffed. "I wouldn't be surprised if your tent caved in and you lost all of your inventory because of it!"

Starman rolled his eyes and scoffed. "Oh, please, man. What you know about ley lines I could write on a penny. Don't you think we pendled the entire area to figure out our location?" He dangled a crystal point pendulum mounted to the end of a thick gold chain. "Besides, this isn't your event, Jack. Caleb said we can sit here and here is where we'll sit!"

Cal walked up and stood next to Morgan. "What's going on?" he asked her.

Morgan shrugged. "You got me. Some sort of psychic showdown."

"Oh, Morgan, dear," Rennie said. "It's nothing, really." She walked over and stood on the other side of her soon-to-be-niece by marriage. "Those two used to be best friends years ago, like brothers. Now look at them." Rennie shook her head. "Every time they're together now, it's about one-upping the other. Ridiculous."

"What happened between them?" Cal asked.

"It's an old story, really. They both went after the L.A. police psychic job and were given a test. After comparing notes, they realized they'd come up with the same answer. Together, they decided to let it go – because how was the department going to choose between them? – but Jack went behind Starman's back and took the job." She sighed and crossed her arms over her chest.

"That wasn't very friend-like," Morgan said.

"It wasn't. But Jack also really needed the money. His family had cut him off when they found out he was working as a psychic. It's been close to forty years. You'd think those two would give it a rest, but Starman felt betrayed and never forgave Jack."

Cal approached the older men. "Hey, you're drawing a crowd. How about you let them get set up, Jack, and you and I will go inside and talk about tomorrow's discussion and book signing?"

Jack, his mouth set in a firm line, said, "Fine." He gave Starman a disgusted look. "I won't be held responsible if your tent is damaged. I tried to help."

"Sure, like you tried to help all those years ago and took that job from me."

At that, Rennie stepped in. "Go on Jack. Go with Caleb." She looked at Starman, hands on hips. "And you. Release it, for goddess's sake. Now go get the boxes out of the van while I finish setting up the tent." He started to protest and she held up a hand. "Morgan will help me with the tent, won't you dear?"

"Let's do this," Morgan said, then stopped to check her phone when it pinged. JJ found some basic information on Jack Steve and Starman McGee and was heading over with the details. She pocketed the phone and grabbed a corner of the tent. Within ten minutes, the top was up, the leg height adjusted, and JJ was walking into the courtyard.

"Starman and I can finish from here," Rennie said, nodded toward JJ as he approached. "Go solve Edna's case. Then you can solve Ian's and move on with your life."

"Who told you about Ian?"

Rennie laughed a little and pointed at her forehead.

"Right," Morgan said. "Let's go, JJ. The preserve awaits."

CHAPTER 10

"WHAT INFO DO YOU HAVE?" Morgan asked as they drove to the campgrounds.

"Some background on Jack and Starman. Jack comes from a wealthy logging family in the U.P. They've never really approved of his line of work. Starman, born Bobby McGee, legally changed his first name in the eighties."

"Bobby McGee? Like the song?"

JJ nodded. "He cited that as the reason for the change. According to the records and what I've cobbled together online, people would stop and ask him to sing it all the time and it was affecting his life in a negative way."

"And he thought Starman was a better choice?"

"Who knows what lurks in the mind of a psychic?" JJ asked.

Morgan shrugged. "Another psychic?"

JJ laughed as he pulled into the campgrounds, only to stop when they both saw the side door on Edna's van wide open.

"What the hell?" Morgan said. They'd secured it as a crime scene and were waiting for a tow truck from Traverse City to take it to impound.

"Probably kids being nosey," JJ said.

Hand on the butt of her holstered gun, Morgan walked on silent feet to the van, JJ close behind. She heard rustling coming from inside the vehicle. "You're not supposed to be in there," she called out. "Show yourself."

A muffled stream of expletives came out ahead of Rocky Banks. He climbed out of the van and stood, barefoot, in the sand in front of them. "What?" he demanded, hands on hips.

"You're not allowed in there," JJ said. He motioned at the broken crime scene tape. "You see that? You've entered an active crime scene and tampered with evidence."

Rocky looked from JJ to Morgan, eyes wide. "I was only retrieving some things that belong to me."

"Such as?" Morgan asked.

The younger man pulled a black bedazzled turban out of his back pocket. "This, for one." He pulled it on. "Now that Edna is gone, I'm a full-fledged psychic now. I deserve the black turban."

Morgan rolled her eyes. "Oh, good lord. What else did you take?" She peered into the van. A few of the built-in drawers were open, clothing shifted about.

"That's it."

"You said things. Plural," JJ said.

Rocky crossed his arms over his chest and stood silent.

"And the inside of the van is definitely not how we left it. JJ, take Rocky on over to the station. Maybe he'll be more inclined to answer our questions down there."

Rocky threw his arms up in the air. "Fine. Fine." He pulled a tarot deck out of the cargo pocket of his pants. "These are *my* cards. Edna promised them to me."

Morgan held out her hand and Rocky placed the deck there. "I'd like to go on the record I don't approve of you touching my deck." He gave her the once over. "You and your unbeliever vibes could screw them up, make them unusable. I'm going to have to do a major clearing on them now."

She ignored him and fanned the deck to make sure there was nothing hidden between the cards. "All clear," she said, handing them back.

"Why are you here?" Rocky asked. "What are you looking for?"

"Just anything we may have missed," JJ said.

"Well, do you want my advice?" Rocky asked.

"Not really, but that probably won't stop you," Morgan replied.

"You're right, it won't." Rocky gestured to the host campsite and pointed to Daisy and Davey's camper. "Those two. They're shady as hell. I wouldn't put murder past them."

"What makes you say that?" Morgan asked. She took a step closer to Rocky and looked at him over the top of her silver aviators. "Did you see or hear something?"

Rocky sifted through tarot deck. "I saw it in my crystal ball. I was doing a reading yesterday, after you found poor Edna's body. Their reflections were all I could see."

"Are you sure they weren't standing near you?" JJ said.

He huffed. "No, it wasn't that sort of reflection. They looked angry."

"You sounded angry last night at the Perch Mouth," Morgan said. "I believe you said Edna was holding you down."

"So what if I did? It's the truth but it doesn't mean I'd kill the old thing. She was grumpy, make no bones about that. And not always a great person. You either liked her or you didn't. I happened to like her, in spite of her nagging ways."

Shouts from the beach drew their attention. "Hey, what's going on over there?" JJ asked.

A little girl, maybe eight years old, was jumping up and down, screaming, "It's Messie! It's Messie! She's here!"

Morgan and JJ exchanged glances then hurried the sixty yards or so over to the beach. At the edge of the water stood a couple of teenagers in wetsuits. Same kids who had picketed the station a couple of months ago, demanding freedom of expression on behalf of their graffiti-producing compatriot. Morgan walked up to them. Miranda Melody Daniels, dressed in her usual black with hair dyed to match, gave Morgan a quick glance out of the corner of her eye. "What do *you* want?"

"What happened?" The crowd was getting louder and louder and Morgan had to shout to be heard over the din.

Miranda shrugged. "It's what the kid there said. Messie just stuck her head up out of the water, did a full roll, then dove back under."

Morgan had grown up in Bijoux with the legends of Messie, the large Loch Ness-type sea monster who inhabited Lake Michigan. She was friendly to swimmers but terrorized the pirates and rum runners of days past. Apparently Messie had a moral code, which Morgan could relate to, but that didn't mean she believed the lake monster was an actual thing. "Does that happen often?"

"Of course not." Miranda huffed. "It's because of climate change."

"How do you figure?"

"Messie likes the slightly warmer part of the lake, around Chicago. But it's too warm down there now because of the shifting thermocline. The fact she's here, this far north along the shoreline, means she's running out of places to live." Miranda shook her head, obviously disgusted. "Law enforcement should already be aware of this threat to both Messie and our world."

"I'm well aware of the conversation around climate change, but Lake Michigan is chilly on a warm day, frigid in the winter. It always has been."

Miranda squared her shoulders. "You are obviously a non-believer. In Messie *and* the climate," she said and stomped away.

Well, that was twice in less than thirty minutes she'd been called a non-believer. She either needed to start having faith in something or work on her poker face. Likely the latter. Lakeside living was evidently softening her.

"It has nothing to do with the water temperature."

Morgan spun around. Rocky was standing about a foot away.

"And what's your theory?" she asked, already knowing the answer.

"It's our psychic presence, of course," Rocky said, crossing his arms over his chest.

JJ groaned.

Rocky continued, "Contrary to what the young lady said, Lake Michigan hasn't changed that much, temperature wise. If anything, it's colder because it's deeper now from increased rain and runoff."

Morgan and JJ stared at him. He shrugged. "What can I say, I wanted to be a marine biologist when I was a kid, before I realized my true calling." He stepped around Morgan, toward the lake, and scanned the horizon. "Messie is here because she feels our loving energy and wants to communicate with us." He turned back to Morgan and JJ. "If it's all right with you, I'd like to head over to the Raven's Nest and let everyone know so we can plan accordingly."

"Plan what exactly?" Morgan asked, hands on hips.

"A vigil, of course." Rocky shook his head. "Honestly, it's like neither of you know anything about the other realms."

"Because we prefer to stay grounded in this one. It's how we solve cases, like your friend's murder," Morgan said.

Rocky paled. His hand flew to his heart. "Maybe Edna is trying to communicate with us through Messie. I hadn't considered that."

Morgan leaned in. "One thing you *can* consider is another visit from one of us if we find out you've taken anything else from the van." She stepped back. "Understood?"

"Who knew that the old witch's death would cause me so much trouble." He looked heavenward. "You know I love you, Edna." He looked back at the officers. "Yes. I understand," Rocky said and trudged off across the dune.

JJ and Morgan stepped away from the crowd. "What are you thinking?" he asked.

"That we don't have any real suspects. We have people who didn't particularly like our victim, but also others who loved her." Morgan rubbed her eyes behind her sunglasses. "Right now, Rocky has been the most vocal. Let's add him to the other searches you're running."

"Copy that." JJ shoved his hands in his pockets. "What do you think about Daisy and Davey? They seemed pretty irritated with Edna for taking over host duties."

"It's a small thing, but sometimes that's enough to set some people off. Sure, might as well check them out too. And then there are the other two psychic murders. I'm surprised no one at the gathering has mentioned those." Morgan scanned the crowd. They were taking their time getting back into the lake, no doubt concerned about potential sea monsters. She turned her attention back to the van. "Let's close up the van and reset the crime scene tape." Morgan checked her watch. "It's after five. I'm going to get some food, see if there's any chatter out there about Edna. I'll grab Griselda from the station afterward and call it a day. How about you?"

"I have those searches running on Jack Steve and Starman McGee. I'll stop by and add Rocky, Davey, and Daisy. Then I need to head home. Hannah is planning a two month anniversary dinner for us. And if I'm late, you'll have another murder on your hands."

CHAPTER 11

MORGAN SAT at the counter at Dave's Deli and ordered a burger, fries, and diet cola. Jerome clucked at her choices. She stared him down until he walked away without saying a word. He brought her pop and she picked up the glass, spinning on the stool to face away from the counter. Good vantage point to see everyone in the deli plus those walking around outside. Mr. Dominic shuffled by, an older woman Morgan didn't recognize on his arm. He might be eighty something and annoying, but apparently he still had moves. *Good for him.*

"What are you thinking?"

Morgan spun toward the voice. Cal had sat down next to her when she was facing the other way. Now they were almost nose to nose. She drew her head back. He smiled. "I can hear your cop brain ticking a mile away." She made a curious face at him. "It's what drew me here tonight. All that ticking. Tick. Tick. Tick."

Morgan laughed and lightly punched him on the arm.

"I like that," he said.

"Being punched? I can arrange for it to happen regularly." Morgan smiled and sipped her drink.

Cal looked from his arm to her. "No. You, laughing. You have a nice laugh."

Their eyes met and her stomach caught. *Nope. Nope. Nope,* Morgan thought and spun back to face the counter.

"But I imagine all the guys tell you that." He picked up the iced tea Jerome had placed on the counter and dropped in a straw. "Like Doc Pete."

"Oh my god. You have to stop with the Doc Pete thing. I get that you're a writer but, seriously, stop trying to create something out of nothing."

"So it's nothing, then?" Cal said. "Huh."

"Not from what I hear," Jerome said as he placed their food in front of them.

"There is absolutely not one thing going on between me and Doc Pete. Aside from him taking care of Griselda." Morgan looked over at Cal's plate. Turkey BLT and fries. "Do you eat here so often that you don't even have to order anymore?"

Cal winked at Jerome. "We have a psychic connection."

"Please." Morgan frowned. "I'm just about psychic-ed out right now."

Jerome laughed and held up his cell as he walked away. "If it makes you feel any better, we also have a magical phone connection."

Morgan held up a fry. "That, I can understand."

Cal picked up his sandwich and took a bite. "Where are we on the case?"

She decided to ignore the 'we.' It would do zero good to, once again, lecture the man on staying out of police business. Morgan had to admit, though, he did have a different take on things than she and JJ did. Made him a pretty darn good sounding board sometimes. *Damn. Okay.* "What's your impression of Rocky Banks?"

"Aside from his unfortunate name?" Cal shrugged. "Eccentric, moody. I noticed several of the other psychics avoided his table area this morning during set up. Heard grumblings of *bad vibes* around him." He dragged a fry through ketchup and popped it in his mouth. "You think he killed Edna?"

"Well, given his rant at the Perch Mouth last night and the conversation I had with him earlier today, I can't discount it." She blew out a breath. "Honestly, I can't discount anyone who looks suspicious right now. Everything I know so far points to one of the psychics as the murderer, but I also feel in my gut I'm missing a big piece of the puzzle." Irritated with herself, she pushed her plate away. "Hey, Jerome? Would you please box this up for me?" Morgan looked at Cal. "I gotta go get Gris and head home. Sleep on this."

Cal nodded. "I get that. Come by the Raven's Nest tomorrow. The psychic fair opens in the morning and Jack Steve is giving his talk at one. Maybe that'll help something click here." He lightly tapped the side of her head and grinned. "Make that brain start ticking again."

CHAPTER 12

"GOOD MORNING," Morgan said as she walked into the small police station the next morning. She let Griselda out of her crate and the cat immediately jumped up on the counter. Morgan leaned against it and scratched her behind the ears. Within a minute, a purr that shook the counter could be heard around the room.

"High test purr there," JJ observed.

"No kidding. It's like a small earthquake." She nuzzled Gris's head then straightened. "So, have your searches turned up anything yet?"

"Actually, yes." JJ walked back to his desk and grabbed his notebook. "I contacted the Traverse City police and talked to the detective on their psychic murder case." He looked up. "They haven't released the info to the public, but the word 'fraud' was scrawled across their victim's hand in black marker. And I emailed Liz. She was able to confirm they found the same on the Detroit victim, this time it was written on the side of a quartz crystal and left in the victim's lap."

"What the hell?" Morgan went to her desk and sat down. "Zoe said something about a crystal the last time she dropped into a trance. That makes three. Same circumstances. Same word. This is not good."

"Someone who has a huge beef with psychics," JJ offered.

"And at the very least, thought these three people were fakes." Morgan grabbed Blossom, the red-headed Powerpuff Girl figure she kept on her desk, and started tossing it up and down. It helped her think. "Why go to a psychic, spend the money, if you don't believe in them? It doesn't make sense." She turned to JJ. "There must be something else, something we're missing."

JJ's computer pinged. He spun his chair around. "I've had a social media search running." He whistled. "Our Mystical Madame Edna Marisol was not very well liked by a lot of her peers and clients."

Morgan walked over to JJ and read over his shoulder. "Edna's divinations are the thing of bad fiction; entirely made up with no storyline."

"Edna needs to fade away to that place where old psychics go. Hell. Hell is where she needs to go. Because that's what she makes my life," JJ read out loud. "Wow." He clicked on the post. "Username *Man in a Turban*."

"And who do we know who wears a turban?" Morgan asked. Okay, granted, there was a lot of turban action going on in town right now. "Who specifically has a tie to Edna?" she added. Morgan checked her watch. "I'm meeting Zoe and Rennie over at Hannah's to talk wedding details. Then I'll go on over to the Raven's Nest and talk to Rocky. The fair starts today and it may prove interesting to see the psychics in their natural habitat."

"Nothing much so far on social media regarding Jack and Starman, beyond them trying to irritate each other. I'll text you if anything usable or damning pops in," JJ said.

The station door chimed. Beau "The Butcher" Cornet, Doc Pete Holz the Veterinarian, and Old Mr. Dominic all came into the station at the same time. Morgan glanced up, certain there was some sort of joke here, but she couldn't quite put her finger on it.

"Oh, Morgan," Beau said as he waved. "It's so nice to see you. You haven't been to the market lately." He eyed her. "You haven't gone vegetarian, have you?" Beau shivered. Meat was his life.

Morgan shivered, too, with the old memory of Beau as her high school boyfriend. He'd played football back then and was in great shape. Now he chopped up meat for a living, had lost a good portion of his hair, and looked like the footballs were now firmly planted around his waist.

"Uh, no, not a veggie. Just haven't had time to do any shopping lately. Murder investigation and all." She eyed Old Man Dominic, who was fast approaching Griselda. Well, fast was relative. "She doesn't like strangers to mess with her," Morgan warned.

"Bull crap," Dominic said as he reached a spotted, bony hand toward the feline.

Griselda puffed her fur and hissed a warning.

The cat and the man stared each other down.

"Well, bull crap to you, too," he said to the cat. He leaned against the counter and Gris jumped up and sauntered to the opposite end.

"Why are all of you here? Did you need something?" Morgan asked. Before they could respond, she added, "And don't even try to tell me you're all psychics now, coming in with predictions about the case."

"Oh, not that I know of," Doc Pete said. "Although, to be honest, I do think I can hear what the animals are thinking sometimes." He frowned. "Mother always said I had an overactive imagination, too many hours spent watching Doctor Dolittle."

Morgan made a mental note to not go out with Pete should the topic ever come up again.

"Anyway, JJ called. Said you needed our help. We're the volunteer deputies." He stepped forward and ran a hand along Griselda's spine. Mr. Dominic glared at him. Pete just smiled. Griselda purred.

Morgan dropped into her desk chair and spun to face her deputy. *"These* are the deputies? Talk to me."

JJ shrugged. "What Pete said."

She raised an eyebrow. "Okay then. You're in charge." She glanced at her watch. "I'll be at Hannah's if you need me."

"WHAT CAN I GET YOU?" Hannah asked from behind the counter.

"Surprise me. Well, surprise me as long as it has something to do with chocolate." Morgan was sitting at the small corner café table next to Zoe and Rennie inside Hannah's Heavenly Confections.

Hannah chuckled and went off to fill Morgan's order. Rennie and Zoe had both ordered before Morgan arrived and were sipping their coffees. A minute later Hannah placed a pink china plate with a cupcake in front of Morgan, along with a latte.

"Well, this ought to keep me energized for the rest of the day," Morgan said, eyeing the chocolatey creation in front of her.

Hannah patted Morgan on the shoulder. "I was thinking of you when I came up with this flavor. Double fudge, caramel filling, sprinkle of sea salt for extra flavor." She wiped her hands on her lime green apron. "I call it Death by Caramel. And the latte has a splash of caramel flavor steamed in with the milk."

Morgan picked up the fork on the side of the plate and took a bite. It was all she could do to keep herself from moaning. Then she gave up and moaned anyway. "Oh my god, Hannah. I call this Death by Amazing," and she took another bite. She looked over at both Zoe and Rennie, who were simply staring at her. "What?"

"Nothing to concern yourself with yet, dear," Zoe said.

"Yet? I don't like the sound of that." Morgan took a sip of the latte and put the fork down. She leaned back in her chair. "Zoe, you said something about a crystal holding the key to Edna's murder. What was that about?"

"I'm sure I don't know. As I've told you before, whatever comes out of a vision is for the person listening to interpret." She took a sip of her herbal tea. "Besides, I rarely remember anything I've said when I'm in that state."

"That seems awfully convenient," Morgan said. "Absolves you of any responsibility."

"Are you here for an interrogation or to help us with the wedding plans?" Rennie asked. "If it's the former, we'll cut you loose. If it's for the wedding, then we have decisions to make."

Morgan sighed. "Fine. Okay." She took another bite of the cupcake and washed it down with a careful drink from the still steaming latte. She folded her hands in her lap and looked at the older women. "What's going on with the wedding and how I can help?"

Rennie and Zoe looked at each other and Morgan swore she could see the thought waves traveling between them. "I have this gorgeous off-white lace dressed picked out at Ava's Dresses, down the street," Zoe said.

"And what's wrong with that?" Morgan asked.

"I think she should be truer to her roots. Off white is not the color witches in our family wear when they get married," Rennie said. "Come to think of it, we never wear that color. It's just, so, basic. Ugh." She wrinkled her nose. "Don't you think so, too, Morgan?" She took Morgan's hands in hers and peered into her eyes.

Morgan's hands tingled. *What the hell?*

Zoe smacked her sister on the arm, breaking the connection. "Knock it off, Ren. You're not going to hypnotize Morgan to get her to agree with you."

Rennie sniffed and leaned back in her chair. "I would never."

"You would always." Zoe looked at Morgan. "Apologies for my sister's behavior."

Eyes narrowed, Morgan took another bite of her cupcake. "How am I supposed to help?"

"Break the tie," Zoe said. "I'll go along with whatever you think."

"Oh, no. That's too much pressure over here. This is your wedding. You do you, not what everyone else tells you to do."

Zoe rested her arms on the table and sighed. "I *am* going for simplicity, and the dress I like *is* a bit fussy. Ava also has an amazing purple silk charmeuse shift that picks up the color of my eyes."

Rennie slapped her hands on her thighs. "Well, there you have it." She flashed a grin at Morgan. "Plus, purple is a good witch color, if you didn't know that."

"I know way more about witches and psychics than I ever wanted to, trust me."

"So, what say you, Morgan?" Zoe asked. "What's your vote?"

"Honestly, I like the idea of purple because I think it would suit you so much better. As long as you love the dress, though. Don't wear anything on your special day you don't love." Morgan's phone pinged and she checked the message. It was from Cal: *You might want to come over. Big argument going on over here.*

"Break in the case?" Zoe asked.

"You know we can help you with that, right?" Rennie added.

Zoe looked over at Rennie. "Morgan doesn't believe in what we do."

"Yes, I caught that vibration, but it never hurts to ask." Rennie shifted in her chair. "Never mind, then."

Morgan sighed and shook her head. "Look, Zoe has gone into a trance in front of me and given information she couldn't have known. I'm trying to be open minded, but you have to understand I worked the fraud squad in the old days. Before moving over to homicide, I saw a lot of what we used to call *bunco*."

"And that's the crux of it, isn't it?" Rennie said. "I wish you could be more open—"

Suddenly, Rennie stopped talking. Her face froze and her eyes glazed over. She stared ahead as though she were looking into the distance.

"What....?" Morgan whispered glancing at Zoe who gave her one of those "we're psychic deal with it" looks. "Where did she go?"

"Hush," Zoe said patting Morgan's hand. "Just listen."

"Fraud. The killer believes but doesn't want to…" Rennie said, her voice a deeper octave than normal. "The killer is conflicted and seeks to honor a promise made. Death ends nothing. Love is always near."

Morgan glanced at Zoe again. "Is this some genetic trait?"

Zoe shrugged. "Well, it does run in the family."

"Okay then." Her phone pinged again. She scanned another message from Cal: *You coming? Or should I call JJ?*

On my way, she texted in response. Morgan leaned back in her chair and blew out a breath.

"Is everything all right?" Zoe said.

"I gotta go. Let me know what else I can help with, though." She gave Rennie a raised eyebrow and squeezed Zoe's hand. "I'm here for you. But, right now, there's a fight at the bookstore. If you want to do something, keep your fingers crossed that we solve this case before we have another murder on our hands."

CHAPTER 13

"*WHAT IS GOING ON HERE?*" Morgan asked as she stepped between Rocky and a psychic she didn't know who were going toe-to-toe. The middle-aged woman angled an arm around Morgan and tried to slap Rocky on the head. Morgan blocked her arm before it connected.

"Rocky didn't do anything wrong," Jimmy the Groupie yelled. He was sitting at Rocky's table. "That old woman over there started it."

The woman turned on Jimmy. "Old? How dare you?" she shouted.

"Stop it now! All of you!" Morgan pointed to a wrought iron bench under the giant oak behind the Raven's Nest. "Have a seat. You," she pointed at the woman and took in her stats. Fifty-ish, tall, thin, silver blonde hair, and a jumble of multi-colored stones hanging around her neck on a silver chain. "Who are you?"

"I'm Janine the All Seeing," she sniffed.

"More like Janine the Pain in the Ass," Rocky grumbled.

Janine made another swing for him. Morgan was tempted to let her follow through, but stopped her at the last minute. She was still a cop, after all. "Janine, why do you want to hit Rocky?" Morgan glanced at the younger man. He was in full-on psychic regalia today, wearing a long, velvet skirt over his denim jumpsuit, a sparkling shawl over his shoulders, and the bedazzled turban he'd pilfered from Edna's van the day before. "Besides the obvious."

"He took *everything* from her."

"Everything from who?" Morgan asked.

"Edna, of course! He's wearing her turban and shawl." She pointed to a table across the yard. "That was the spot where Edna was going to set up her table. She turned back to Rocky whose hands were gripping tightly onto a sequined purple satchel. And inside that purse is Edna's prized tarot pack. It's obvious he killed her so he could take over her clients. Edna was my friend and I will not stand for it!"

Rocky rolled his eyes. "Whatever, Janine." He pulled the shawl tighter around his shoulders and adjusted the turban. "Edna promised all of this stuff to me." He crossed his legs and leaned back. "So, you know, your word against mine."

Morgan blew out a breath. "Accusing someone of murder is not something I take lightly. Do you have any proof, other than Rocky here annoys you?"

"Well, I did see him coming out of Edna's van the night she died. I'm staying at the site on the other side of him. He was wearing all blue jean stuff, like he always does." Janine's eyes filled with tears. "Why'd you do it, Rocky? I know Edna was pretty darn horrible to you sometimes, but to kill her like that...."

"And you're just now telling me this?" Morgan interjected.

"I saw it too." Morgan turned at the voice. It was Davey. "Didn't really think much of it since Edna was mentoring him and all. But now that Janine mentions it, it could seem suspicious." He rubbed his chin and stared at Rocky.

Rocky jumped to his feet. "Oh hell no. I am not going down for this." He turned and started to stomp off, but Morgan grabbed his arm. He spun around and glared at her.

"Morgan?"

She glanced over her shoulder. Cal had parted the crowd and was standing behind her. "Caleb," she said.

"Sorry I had to leave for a few, had to get Jack settled." He looked Rocky, Davey, and Janine over. "Interesting party you have going on here. Maybe we can take it somewhere more private so as not to disturb the patrons?"

"Exactly what I was thinking," Morgan replied. "Mind if Rocky and I use one of your rooms to have a nice, quiet chat?" The Raven's Nest housed several "secret meeting rooms" used for card playing and drinking during prohibition. Morgan discovered while investigating the last murder in Bijoux that at least one of them had a secret entry.

"Help yourself. I actually cleaned out and freshly painted the second one on the left last week. Turned it into a little conference room."

"Perfect."

"Jack's still in the store, getting ready for his talk, FYI." Cal glanced at his watch then addressed the crowd. "You're all welcome inside for Jack Steve's book presentation and signing. We begin in about twenty minutes, at one o'clock." Those gathered around started dispersing back to their tables, continuing readings that had been interrupted by the commotion of the dueling psychics or heading inside.

"Have a seat," Morgan said to Rocky as they entered the small work room. "What's going on with you?" she asked as she closed the door behind him. The room was small, about eight foot by eight foot, but the walls were whitewashed and the lighting was bright, so it felt larger. "Talk to me."

Rocky crossed his arms and leaned back in his chair. It was wood and creaked under the movement. "It's obvious you already believe I'm guilty. I have nothing to say."

Morgan leaned forward and rested her elbows on the old cherry table. "You can take that tact, or you can tell me your side of the story."

"I've already done that. Edna was sometimes horrible. Sometimes nice. She kept me under her thumb, refused to set me free, said my abilities reflected on hers since she was my mentor." He sucked in a breath and blew it out. "Overall, I didn't like her. But, you know, you can dislike people and not actually murder them. And that's all I'm saying. If you're not going to cut me loose, I want a lawyer." Rocky blinked back the tears rimming his eyes.

For not saying anything, he'd certainly said quite a bit. She *almost* felt sorry for him. *Damn.* Lakeside living was definitely softening her up. There was a time when she was suspicious of everyone, believed maybe a tenth of what any suspect told her, was always ready to arrest the guilty and defend the innocent.

Maybe it wasn't such a bad thing to be losing some of her cynicism. This was a small town, after all, with its own personality and quirks. She was a good cop, but it didn't hurt to switch perspective once in a while.

"Okay, Rocky. It's safe to assume your prints are all over Edna's van, so no sense going there. Here's what I'm going to do. I'm going to run your information through the databases. And I'm waiting for some DNA testing. You come down to the station for a swab, continue to cooperate, and if you don't match, you can go on your way. In the meantime, please don't leave Bijoux."

"I can't leave. I don't have much money. I need to get back out to the fair so I can earn some cash for gas and food." He relaxed a little, though still obviously distressed. "I promise I won't leave without talking to you and I'll go down to the station for a test."

"Thank you." Morgan opened the door to leave. "You coming along?"

Rocky shook his head. "I need a few to collect myself."

Morgan closed the door behind her and walked out to the back deck. She scanned the tables of readers and their clients. Everything seemed to be running without issue now. Jimmy had moved onto another reader. The Garanimal guy from the bar was listening intently to whatever Starman was telling him. Even Janine, whose table was near the door, had settled into giving a palm reading to Doc Pete. Pete waved at her. She offered what she hoped was her best I-like-you-but-not-in-that-way smile and went back into the store and the crowd gathered for Jack Steve's book discussion. "Is that fresh coffee I smell?" she said to Cal as she maneuvered through the book stacks and approached the counter.

Cal filled a mug and handed it to her. She inhaled and took a sip. "You do make good coffee, Professor Joseph."

He smiled. "It was one of my minors in college."

Morgan gestured with the mug toward the front of the shop, where Jack was leaning on a podium and talking loudly. Did the man have a volume switch? If so, she'd love to find it. Even the spectators shouted out their questions. *He must bring that out in others. Some people have that unfortunate superpower.* "How goes the talk? Aside from the noise, looks like you have a decent crowd." She glanced out the side window where it opened on the courtyard. "For both events. Should be good for sales."

"True and it is. But you're not here to talk about any of this." He leaned on the counter and looked at her over the top of his black horn-rimmed glasses. "I hear the ticking."

Morgan sighed. "Fine. Tell me what happened between Janine and Rocky before I got here."

"A lot of yelling and finger pointing. Mostly by Janine toward Rocky. She even tried to pull the turban off Rocky's head." Cal shook his head and took a sip of coffee. "They were really going at it, which is when I texted you. They finally started to settle down right after that, so I thought it'd be safe to come inside and get Jack set up." He nodded toward the speaker, who was just finishing up.

"And that's the story of how I solved the case of the San Francisco Strangler back in the 80's." Jack Steve concluded his talk on his latest book, *Death by the Bay,* to a round of applause. He held up both hands. "Thank you, so much." He placed a hand over the center of this chest. "It does this old heart good to know so many of you are out there, fighting the good fight in the name of psychics everywhere." He glanced around the room. "Even you non-psychics." He winked and the crowd laughed. "Us sensitive types need all the support we can get." He stepped down from the dais and meandered through the crowd, greeting well-wishers on his way to the counter where Morgan and Cal were standing.

"Jack! Oh, Jaaaaaack!" Daisy called out as she and Davey hurried over. "Would you please do us the honor of signing our copy of *Psychics in Love.*" She handed the well-worn book, along with a pen, to Jack. "We know you wrote it about us and can't thank you enough. It makes us so happy." She beamed at Davey.

"What?" Jack asked. "I'm sorry, but do I know you?"

Daisy tapped his arm playfully and giggled. "Of course, you do, silly. How else could you have told our story? This is Davey Rocket and I'm Daisy."

"Yeah, we don't look the same as we did forty years ago. Time'll do that to you," Davey added.

"Davey and Daisy." Jack rubbed his mustache for a moment, then recognition lit his eyes. "We met at a Dead concert, didn't we? You had a booth set up next to mine and Zoe's."

"That's right." Daisy smiled. "We told you our story, then years later you wrote this wonderful book about our adventures."

"Well, I'm so sorry to have to tell you this, Daisy, but *Psychics in Love* is about my personal adventure with Zoe Buffett." He smiled warmly. "You remember Zoe, don't you?"

Morgan leaned toward Cal and whispered, "I'll be needing a copy of that."

Cal nodded. "I got you covered."

"I remember her. But oh. Oh my," Daisy said, frowning. "We were just so certain...."

Davey squeezed her hand. "Never forget, my love, all of our stories are part of the collective consciousness. Shared across time and space. His and Zoe's story *is* our story, too."

"Absolutely." Jack nodded, still smiling. He signed the book and handed it back. "Thank you for being here. There's still much more for you to do in this world. Keep being a lighthouse of love for the masses, okay?"

Daisy and Davey beamed at Jack but Morgan noticed the woman's eyes narrow as Jack turned his back to speak to a fan.

"How about my copy? Will you sign it, too?" a man asked walking up to the gathering crowd around them.

Morgan turned around. It was the Garanimal guy. Today he was wearing black jeans and a black dachshund rescue t-shirt with white lettering. Who knew dachshunds needed rescuing? And what was his name? She searched her memory. For a cop, she was terrible with names. "Elvis, right?"

"Elvis? Who's named Elvis. Besides the King, of course." The guy bristled. "It hasn't been that long since we met. You're not good with this cop stuff, are you? I'm *Trent*. Not Elvis."

"Feeling a little edgy there, *Trent*?" Morgan asked. She took a closer look at him.

He looked away. "I'm fine, just probably need some more coffee."

That Morgan could understand.

Trent turned to Jack. "I'd like my book signed, if you don't mind."

Jack held out his hand and Trent handed over the book. "Would you like it inscribed to you? Or just autographed?"

Trent didn't answer right away.

"I'm waiting to talk to Jack, so decide. Now," Morgan said. "Or lose your chance."

"Fine, fine. Just sign it. Did you know autographed books are more valuable if they're not made out to an individual?" He looked at Morgan and frowned. "What is up with you? Are you always this grumpy and irritable? Have *you* had enough coffee today?"

"I am not grumpy," Morgan said, eyes narrowed. "But I am getting irritated."

"I'm flattered you think my book will be worth something some-day." Jack handed the signed book back to the other man.

"You should get help for your anger issues. It might help if you smiled more, too," Trent said to Morgan. He held the book up. "Thanks," he said as he walked away.

"He did not just tell me to smile," Morgan said. She looked at Cal, who was trying not to laugh, when a man shouted near the back of the store.

The crowd went silent and Morgan and Cal ran toward the sound. The young man was standing outside the room where Morgan had spoken with Rocky. Rocky was still at the table except he was face down with his tarot cards spread out in front of him.

CHAPTER 11

MORGAN RUSHED into the room as she pulled on a pair of nitrile gloves from her back pocket. "Cal call for an ambulance!" she shouted. Morgan leaned over and checked for a pulse on Rocky Banks's neck. Nothing. She noted the bruising on the side that was visible to her. Similar to Edna, she thought. Possibly from a rope. "Never mind the ambulance. Call Doc McVie instead."

How the hell did this happen with all of these people around? WHILE I WAS AROUND? She looked at her watch. It had been about forty minutes since she spoke to him in the meeting room. She looked up. Cal was pale. "Cal, take a breath."

She turned to the man. "What's your name? And what were you doing in this area?"

He swallowed and his gaze skittered away from Rocky, but his eyes kept darting back and forth between him and Morgan.

"Sir?" Morgan said.

"I just wanted to use the bathroom."

"Did you see anyone? Near this room?"

"No, no one." He took a deep breath and Morgan could see he was trying to settle his nerves.

"What's your name?"

"This is my son, Rob McGee," Starman said as he draped a protective arm around the younger man's shoulder. He looked past Morgan. "Shame about Rocky there. I told him to be careful."

"Dad…." Rob began.

"Rob here is like you, Captain. Another naysayer. Started out as a lawyer." He glanced at his son. "Doesn't believe anything about what his old man does. Now the dude writes about it."

"Tell me about that," Morgan said.

"It's a side job. I'm an investigative reporter for *Out of the Shadows*. We're an online magazine. Our focus is debunking psychic phenomena. It's why I'm here this weekend."

"And to see your dear dad," Starman added.

Rob grimaced. *No love lost there*, Morgan thought. "So, you think this is all fake?"

"Fraudulent would be the word. These people prey on those with lesser minds."

Fraud. Bells went off in Morgan's head. "Wow. Okay." JJ entered the small room and Morgan nodded at him as she stepped to the side. Morgan handed Rob a piece of paper. "Write down your contact info, Rob. Please hang around. I'll have more questions as soon as we get Rocky here settled."

"Doc McVie will be here in a few," JJ said.

"Okay, then. Let's get this processed." She turned to the gathered crowd. "Please, everyone, step back. Go to your tables. Do whatever it is you were doing before this happened. But do not leave the premises, we will be questioning all of you regarding this matter."

"How can I help?" Cal asked. He ran a hand through his thick black hair and started pacing. "This is just horrible."

Morgan sighed. "Murder always is." She put a hand on his shoulder to stop his pacing. "See to your guests, make sure no one leaves. And be ready for questioning after JJ and I finish up."

"Questioning? Seriously, Morgan. You can't think I had anything to do with this."

"Of course not. You were with me. I want to talk about the attendees."

Cal stopped and closed his eyes. "Okay. That I can do."

"Thank you," Morgan said. She looked around the room. The walls seemed solid. But it was an old building and from Morgan's experience getting locked in by Connie a few months back – there were nooks and crannies that even Cal probably hadn't yet discovered. The town wasn't short on rumors of underground tunnels used by rum runners and pirates, leading all the way from Lake Michigan to some of the older buildings. If the stories were true, there could very well be a hidden tunnel running underneath the bookstore. "You recently remodeled this room. Find any secret entrances in the process? Anything where another person could slip in and out?"

He shook his head. "No. Unlike some of the rooms, this one seems to be solid."

"Okay. Please go herd your psychics and keep an eye out for anyone acting strange. Janine in particular since she and Rocky were just fighting. Though I don't think she'd be strong enough to strangle someone."

Cal lifted an eyebrow.

Morgan rolled her eyes. "Okay, stranger than usual." She turned back to find Rob still standing outside the room. "How about you go have a seat at your dad's table outside." She nodded toward the back door. "JJ will take a written statement when we're finished here."

"A statement? I don't know why you'd need anything else from me." He sniffed, suddenly defensive. "After all, from what I've observed, *you* were the last person to see him alive." Rob glared at Morgan. "Maybe you did it."

"Now hold on a minute," Morgan said. She was well aware of the propensity of lawyers to shift blame, though it was usually so their clients would seem innocent, not themselves.

"That's an interesting idea. The murders *did* start when you returned to Bijoux, Morgan Hart. Perhaps you refuse to discuss the possibility of a Detroit Killer because you *are* the Detroit Killer."

Morgan didn't bother to look behind her. "You got here awfully damn fast this time, Connie. Monitoring the police scanner?"

"Just happened to be near the station when I saw JJ run out the door. Thought it would be prudent to follow him. Turns out it was. You just can't discount a good reporter's instinct." She pulled her cell phone out of her pocket and Morgan assumed she was switching on the video camera in the phone.

Morgan held up her hand. "Do not film this. We haven't processed the scene, let alone had any time to notify the family."

"As the killer, I'd think you'd already know what happened here." Connie nodded toward the body and frowned. "Though I do suppose you have to continue the ruse for the sake of appearances."

"Exactly what I was thinking," Rob said. He extended a hand to

Connie. "Rob McGee, lawyer and investigative reporter of so-called psychics."

Connie shook his hand. "Interesting. I obviously overheard your theory that Morgan here killed poor Rocky. I like it."

"Of course you do," Morgan said. "How about you both move along?"

The bookstore crowd started murmuring. "The police captain might be the killer," they whispered. "Detroit Killer." "Murderer right here in front of us." "Don't be alone with her."

"Unbelievable!" Jack boomed. "Inconceivable!"

Unbelievable and inconceivable, yes, Morgan thought. *Obviously these psychics were way off their supposed game if they thought she was the killer.* She approached Connie and whispered, "If you honestly believe I'm capable of such a thing, then you may want to back off."

Connie smirked, but took a step back and slipped her phone back in her pocket.

Morgan turned to Jack. "What are you bellowing about?"

"The very thought this could happen while I was here in the store and didn't pick up on the break in the psychic connection we all share." He made a sweeping gesture with his hand and several people ducked out of the way. "There's been a break in the continuum and it was, somehow, masked to all the psychics gathered here." He squinted at Morgan. "What type of witch are you?"

"What are you talking about? I'm not a witch."

"Please, I smelled witch on you the second we met." He squinted his eyes. "And one of those who are in denial of their innate talents." Still squinting, he looked her up and down. "Obviously quite angry about it, too. Your subconscious witch-self has forced you to act out against this poor young man in order to get attention."

Morgan just stared at him. *What the hell?*

"Morgan, I do believe this is the first time I've seen you at a loss for words," Cal said, his lips quivering.

She gave him one of her icy stare-downs. In return Cal bit his lip and cleared his throat. He looked like he was doing all he could not to burst out laughing.

"It's because she's guilty and both Rob and Jack just called her out on it," Connie said, smiling up at the older man. "Hey! JJ!" she called out to the deputy.

JJ stuck his head out the work room door. "What do you want, Connie?"

"You need to open an independent investigation into Morgan here. She obviously can't investigate herself. Conflict of interest." Connie's lip curled. "Though I can imagine that's exactly something a killer would try to do."

JJ ignored the reporter. "Hey, Cap'n, if you're done being accused of murder, there's something in Rocky's hand. You might want to take a look."

Morgan shook her head at the inanity and entered the room. JJ pointed to Rocky's right hand. It was balled up into a fist. "It looks like a piece of thick paper."

She gently extricated the item and unfolded it. A tarot card. More specifically, The Fool. With 'FRAUD' scrawled across it in black marker. She stepped away from the table and angled the card in the overhead light. "It looks like there might be a finger or thumb print on here, lower left corner, smudged maybe under the marker," Morgan noted. "Let's see if we can pull a clear enough image to run through the databases."

JJ opened an evidence bag and Morgan dropped the card in. She considered Rocky while they waited for the M.E. "He certainly wasn't a happy person, no money, riding on Edna's coattails. With her death he seemed to think he could really make a go of it."

"I guess someone else had other ideas," JJ said quietly, so only Morgan could hear. "And we considered him a suspect."

"That we did. I suppose he still could be. Except that would mean..."

"Two killers on the loose," JJ whispered away from the onlookers. "What are the odds of that?"

"Extremely slim." She noticed Connie was retreating, which meant Doc McVie must have arrived "And one I'm not ready to consider. For now, we'll put Rocky in the 'disgruntled friend' category. And let's add Rob McGee to the list of people of interest. He used the word 'fraud' when he spoke about psychics."

McVie arrived, medical bag in hand, and directed Maggie toward the body. "Wow," was all he said when he stood over Rocky.

"Yeah," Morgan said.

AN HOUR AND A HALF LATER, Morgan and JJ stepped back as Doc McVie removed Rocky's body from the Raven's Nest. "I'll send you my initial findings later today," he said as he got into the ambulance/M.E. vehicle. He motioned for Morgan and she approached the driver's window. "You know I don't like to speculate, but I'd say same manner of death as our first victim, on first inspection anyway." He turned the key in the ignition. "I did find some DNA on Edna's neck. No idea if it's hers or not. Sent it in, just so you know. No word yet on that. Might not be until Tuesday or later in the week, with the holiday weekend and all."

Morgan patted the side of the vehicle and stepped back. "Thanks, Doc." She turned and surveyed the scene before her. About thirty psychics had set up at various tables around the deck and courtyard behind the bookstore. They seemed quiet now, already resuming readings. Morgan was certain they were reassuring clients that they would, indeed, find love, happiness, and success. She shook her head. Maybe quiet wasn't quite the right word. There was a palpable undercurrent of tension, which was to be expected. Two of their own had been murdered over the span of two days. Any one of them could be next.

JJ walked over and whispered, "You're considering the psychic serial killer angle now, aren't you?"

"As much as I hate to go there, it's hard not to. This makes four deaths in the past three months. Two here. On our shift. And it stops now." She ground out the words. "Do you have the volunteer deputies lined up to begin patrol?"

"That I do. Beau is taking the night shift this evening. He'll drive around until about midnight. Then Mr. Dominic will take first part of the day, because he can't see at night and Pete will pick up any slack in the afternoon. They'll be in later today to go over the game plan. We should be covered."

"Sounds good. While you're sorting through the items we just gathered, I'll go question Caleb Joseph about his psychic attendees."

CAL WAS STANDING behind the large carved oak counter when Morgan entered the store. He raised his mug in greeting, then poured her a cup of coffee and motioned to the two overstuffed black leather chairs arranged in front of the river rock fireplace. "We may as well be comfortable while you question me."

Morgan took a sip and considered him over the rim of the mug. Last time this happened, when he'd discovered the body of a fellow romance writer at the Firefly, he'd been a lot more flustered. But then, he *had* extracted the knife which had killed her, leaving his prints all over it, marking himself a prime suspect. "You don't seem nervous."

"Of course, I'm nervous. And I'm sad. But mostly I'm furious. Why the hell does this keep happening?"

"I wish I knew." She touched his arm. His muscles were hard, tense, as were his eyes. She knew that look. He was ready to jump at any moment and start his own investigation.

"I'm almost—almost, mind you—willing to consider Connie's theory of a Detroit Killer," Cal said. He set his cup down and leaned forward, his elbows on his knees. "Not the one about you being the murderer, of course, but the overall idea of it." His eyes stared intently into hers.

She dropped her hand and sat back. *Too close for comfort.* "You're being as ridiculous as Connie."

"Am I? No murders in almost a century until you move back to town." He studied the back of his hands and shrugged. "I'm sorry, but you *are* a link. You can't deny it."

"You're not sorry and I'm not a link. You're diverting attention from the fact that you've hosted two events and both have resulted in people being murdered, Caleb."

"Maybe." He sighed. "I'm not sure about any of this. Okay go ahead and grill me. What do you want to know?"

Morgan looked around her. Under different circumstances, it'd be a cozy scene. Two friends talking about books over a cup of coffee. Her chest constricted and she realized she missed the intimacy of deep conversation with another human. A partner in life, actually. She shook off the melancholy and pulled out her notebook and pen. "Did you see Rocky after I left him? Maybe when I walked outside? See anyone walk into the room after me?"

He shook his head. "No, but I was also focused on Jack and the crowd. I did run upstairs to my apartment for a few minutes, so I wasn't here the whole time."

"Your flat upstairs has windows facing the courtyard, right? Did you happen to look out? See anything odd?"

"I didn't go near the window. I grabbed the portable charger for my phone off the kitchen counter and came right back down."

"Did you have anyone upstairs with you who may have seen something?"

"You know I don't make it a habit of taking people upstairs." He raised an eyebrow. "If you want to know if I'm dating someone, all you have to do is ask."

"Well, that was a leap." Morgan bristled, which quickly folded into curiosity. He never talked about that sort of stuff. "Are you? Dating someone, that is?"

She watched Cal entertain a smile. "I'm not. And I haven't for quite a while if that's going to be your second question. And they've all ended amicably, if that's your third, so no one's out to frame me or anything like that."

She laughed a little. "That went off course pretty damn quick."

"I've been around you long enough to know how your thoughts run. Tick, tick, tick, remember?" He took a drink of coffee. "Plus, I've been researching investigations. You know, since I'm going to write a mystery next. Of course, it'll be under my own name. Josie Steele only writes gothic romances."

She'd secretly read some of 'Josie's' books. They were surprisingly good, but she inwardly agreed that particular style definitely wouldn't lend itself to stories about murders and police work. "You writers hardly ever get anything right about what us cops and detectives do."

Morgan tapped her pen on her notebook. "So, tell me? What am I going to ask you next?"

"If I've heard any chatter among the group out there."

She didn't like that he could read her so well. She half shrugged. "Okay, I'll give you that. And have you?"

"They're handing out predictions to each other like cookies. Everyone has a theory and they're all different, with one exception. Each believes there's a psychic serial killer on the loose."

"Two murders don't make a serial killer."

"No, but some of them knew about Traverse City and a couple more knew about Detroit. It doesn't take much to put two and two together. Last I heard, they were predicting each other's deaths."

"Who does that?"

"A group of psychics, that's who."

Cal and Morgan swung around in their seats. Jack Steve was standing behind them. "How long have you been there?" Morgan asked.

"Long enough to know my esteemed host needs help with his love life."

"I do not need help."

Jack waved a hand. Morgan poked Cal on the arm. "Says you," she said. She looked at Jack. "Do you carry love spells around with you when you're eavesdropping?"

"It wasn't my intent to listen in. I came to get the extra copies of my book that I left here earlier. And to talk to both of you."

"So, talk. Unless you're going to continue accusing me of murder. And being a witch." Morgan flicked her hand at Jack. "If that's all you have, you can go."

"What does the word 'fraud' have to do with your investigation?"

Morgan felt her entire body go on alert. She stared at him for a few moments assessing this new zinger. "Why would you ask me that?"

"It's obvious you don't believe in what I do, but that particular word keeps coming to mind." He walked over to the bay window and looked out at the gathering of readers and their clients.

Morgan followed his gaze. A ring of tea light candles had been arranged around Rocky's table.

"And," Jack continued, still staring out the window, "there are enough folks like you, non-believers, who would consider what we do to be fraudulent."

Like Starman's son, Morgan thought. "I'm not here to judge," Morgan said, flipping her notebook closed and slipping the pen into the metal spiral. "I'm here to keep everyone safe and prevent anything else bad from happening." She carried her empty coffee cup over to the pot behind the counter and set it down. "To that end, I'm heading back to the station."

"I'll be over later," Cal said. "I have those treats for Griselda."

"Good. She's going to need them after I tell her about Rocky."

CHAPTER 15

JJ's COMPUTER pinged as Morgan entered the police station. He tapped on the keyboard and kept his eyes on the screen. "I was able to pull a partial print from the tarot card we found in Rocky's hand. Dropped it into the database when I got back. Just got a hit."

Morgan dropped into her desk chair. "Who is it?"

"Dammit."

She rarely heard him swear. "That bad?"

"It's not good." JJ replied. "The data points to a juvenile record. Sealed here in Michigan, years ago. All this time passed. I'm surprised it wasn't expunged." He stood up and started pacing.

She motioned toward his computer. "So, open it up, let's see who it is."

"Normally, we could do that. But because it's been officially sealed by a judge, a court order is required to open the file. I've only seen this a few times before, when a juvenile had committed a felony." He looked at her. "Or a more heinous crime."

"I know it's Saturday, but if we can find a judge who's willing, we may be able to get them to sign the paperwork. Especially given the circumstances." Morgan's mind went blank for a second. "Wait. Do we have a judge? I just realized I don't know."

JJ grimaced. "The mayor. He's also the judge."

"What? How did I not know that?"

"I guess because we haven't needed one until now." JJ printed out the information, along with a release form, and handed it to Morgan. "Maybe you can get him to sign this when you give him an update on the case?"

She eyed her deputy. "Coward."

"That I am. I do not wish to tangle with Mayor Ed. He's been making veiled threats to Hannah to get her building updated *or else.* I'd rather not rock that particular boat and cause her any more stress." He sat down. "Having said that, you do know I would never let anything like this interfere with my duty, right?"

"Of course, I know that. You're a great cop." She walked over to his desk and patted his shoulder. "Keep digging. Anything turned up yet on our coastal psychic visitors, Jack Steve or Starman McGee? Something about them doesn't add up in my mind."

"I think you like saying 'coastal." JJ chuckled. "Another vibe?"

"Not quite a vibe." Morgan frowned. "More of a gut thing, like I've eaten something that hasn't quite settled and won't until we solve this case."

"Gotcha. Nothing so far on Starman or Jack beyond normal social media interactions. Promos, bios, reviews."

"Any of those reviews go off the rails, like Edna's?"

"Some, but nothing that has *me* vibing." He smiled at her. "They do have a fairly consistent pattern of sniping at each other, though."

"Yeah, I got to see that in person at Cal's earlier." She filled him in on the decades old rivalry. "It's sad that anyone would let a friendship go over something like a job." Morgan sighed. "Apparently all the psychic inner workings have affected Starman's relationship with his son as well. Let's add Rob McGee to our search list. He used the word 'fraudulent' when he talked about the psychics earlier today."

"That's interesting." JJ turned back to this computer. "I'm on it. I'll let you know."

"Okay. I'm off to talk to Mayor Ed. I'll take this one for the team, but the next one is yours."

JJ nodded. "Fair enough."

MORGAN LEFT the station and pulled out her cell phone, readying to call the mayor, when she heard his unmistakable roar coming from down the street. She found him standing in front of the Perch Mouth Bar and Grille, arguing with Frankie.

"Everything okay here?" she asked.

Frankie put her hands on her hips and frowned. "He's telling me I have to fix this place up on the outside." She stared at the mayor. "I don't have that kind of money. And even if I did, I wouldn't change the bar. It has lakeside charm."

Mayor Ed snorted. "Charm? All the charm of a dump!" He swung his beefy arm to point at the building. "You and the other Hold Outs are keeping Bijoux in the dark ages. Peeling paint, stained shingles, wood siding pulling apart." He made a face. "I mean, just look at it. You have to see the disrepair."

"As I said, I like the disrepair." Frankie stood feet braced apart, trading him glare for glare. "There's nothing unsafe about it. I've had the code inspector here to make sure. And I like it just as it is."

He stared back. "You, and the rest of the shopkeepers like you, will be the death of this town."

The argument was drawing a crowd and Morgan decided it was time to put an end to it. "Let's call it a stand-off for now." She turned to the mayor. "I need to talk to you. Mind grabbing a table inside with me?"

"What makes you think I want him in there?" Frankie asked.

"Please let it go for the moment, Frankie."

Frankie threw up her hands. "Whatever," and walked back into her bar.

Mayor Ed let out a breath. "I honestly do like this place. I love this entire town. I'm only trying to make it better."

"I get that. Your crusade might go further, though, if you didn't insult the business owners." She opened the door and they grabbed a table by the front window. Morgan waved off the waitress. "We won't be here that long."

"What do you need to discuss? Do you have leads on the murder?"

"It's murders, now. Plural."

"What the hell? When did this happen?" He slammed his hand on the table and caught the attention of the other patrons.

Morgan glanced around the room, then whispered, "Please, can we keep it down? It happened just this afternoon so we're still waiting for Doc McVie to confirm the cause of death."

Mayor Ed leaned back in his chair. "Another psychic?"

Morgan nodded. "Rocky—Rockefeller Banks. He was the first victim's friend and protégé. We found out there have been two other psychics killed in the state with the same M.O. over the past three months. One in Traverse City and one in Detroit. That information is on a need to know basis, though it seems some of the psychics have already figured it out."

"Predicted it, did they?"

Morgan shook her head and chuckled. "If they were that good, they'd have known death was coming for them. Right?"

"Maybe. Who knows what lurks in the mind of a psychic? I had a reading with one of them. It was obtuse, to say the least." He leaned forward again, resting his arms on the table.

"Yeah, that's my experience, too. What did they tell you?"

"That I won't be mayor much longer." He laughed out loud. "Can you imagine? No one wants this job, it's how I got it in the first place." He motioned to the waitress and ordered a cheeseburger and fries, along with a Diet Coke. He looked at Morgan and she shook her head. "So, what are you doing about this? We have to keep the town safe. And I don't need to remind you again..."

"It's an election year. Yes, I know. We've called in the volunteer deputies to do nighttime patrols around town and out at the Preserve." She pulled the paperwork for the release of records out of her pocket. "And I need you to sign these. We got a hit on a partial fingerprint, but it's a sealed juvenile record. It requires a court order to release it to us."

"That's unusual. Law enforcement usually has rights to open these cases." Mayor Ed glanced at the papers. "I need to read through these before I can sign them. I'll bring them over to you when I'm done reviewing the details."

"Please keep in mind this is an urgent matter. The psychics leave Monday. This could be our only chance to capture the killer." She leaned back in her chair. "I would think you'd be in a hurry, this being an election year and all."

"Do not lecture me." He waved the papers. "Opening a juvenile record which has been sealed like this requires careful consideration. I've been an attorney and judge for more years than I've been a mayor, so you're just going to have to deal with it."

Morgan pushed herself up from the table. "Fine. Call me when you're ready." She walked out the door and back to the station.

"How'd it go?" JJ asked when Morgan returned to the station

"He's going to *consider* it. Can you believe that?" She picked up Griselda from the counter and buried her face in the cat's fur. The purr that shook the earth began again.

"Considering what she's been through, that is one chill cat."

Morgan turned when the door opened behind her. She recognized the three people entering from the psychic orientation at the Firefly and the fair, though she hadn't met them yet.

A tall thin man with long blond hair, mid-forties, stood in the middle of the group. "I'm Sven the Seer. We're on a short break from the fair."

"And?" Morgan said.

"We—all of us," he gestured to the others, "have information on the case."

A short woman wearing a lacy shawl and long velvet dress stepped forward. "Griselda has been calling out to me. She's very worried about Edna and Rocky." Her eyes teared as she looked at the cat Morgan was still cradling. "Those two can't cross over until they know this little soul is cared for."

"I have a hard time believing Rocky is worried. He didn't care all that much for Griselda," Morgan said. "But you should know that."

Sven stepped between Morgan and the other psychic. "Be that as it may, Edna and Rocky are also both understandably angry. They don't think you're doing a very good job of finding their killer," he added.

Morgan put Griselda back down on the counter. She stepped forward, hands on hips, eyes narrowed. "Do they now?" She eyed the group. "Considering Rocky just died, he should have a little patience. Have either of them told you who did it? All this information you claim to have, do one of you have an ID of the killer?" she demanded.

JJ walked over to Morgan. He placed a hand on her arm. "What the captain means is thank you for the information. We're doing our best."

Morgan shook off his hand and dropped her arms to her side. What was she doing, arguing with a bunch of psychics? Holy crap, she really was losing it. "Anything else?" she asked, her tone daring them to speak.

The third person, a man who had been standing behind the other two, stepped forward. He took Morgan's hands in his. She resisted, but he held tight. "Ian loved you more than anything, Fay, but you need to let go," was all he said, then released her hands. "It's not safe. Let it *all* go."

Morgan stood there, dumbstruck, as they filed back out the door. "Dammit," she finally said. "I really hate psychics."

As the group left, Beau, Doc Pete, and Mr. Dominic, the volunteer deputies, walked in.

"Might as well put a revolving door into the budget for later this year," Morgan said to JJ.

"Yeah, no kidding."

Caleb entered behind them and took in the group. "If I'd known there was going to be a party, I would've brought a cake."

Morgan went over to the counter. "These are the volunteer deputies."

Cal considered them. They considered him back. He shrugged. "And a fine group they are."

Morgan started to retort, when Mr. Dominic interrupted, "You kissed that girl yet?" he asked Cal, motioning to Morgan with his cane.

Cal choked. "Excuse me?"

"Oh, everybody at the senior center knows you got the hots for this here chickie."

"You did not just call me chickie."

Undaunted, Mr. Dominic continued, "We have a pool going." He rubbed his hands together. "Come to think of it, if you kiss her now, I'll win."

"I am a gentleman; I do not kiss and tell, nor do I kiss to fulfill bets."

"There's my stuffy professor," JJ said from his desk. "I wondered when he was going to show up."

"I am not stuffy. I have morals. And affection is a private thing."

Morgan snorted. "Really? So you don't hold hands in public? No PDA for you?" She looked him over. "Are you actually human, or a robot trying to be a real boy?"

Griselda howled from her end of the counter. Cal shot Morgan a squinty look, then turned his focus to the cat. "*She's* the only reason I'm here," he said and dropped a bag of treats on the counter. He pulled a few out. Gris scurried over and inhaled them. "Good kitty," he muttered as he scratched her ears. "Unlike these humans, who are not so good."

"For heaven's sake, get over yourself," Morgan said. "You're such a professor."

"Will there be kissing or not?" Beau asked. "If so, I volunteer." He eyed Morgan up and down and smiled his toothy smile. "Not like it'd be the first time we locked lips."

Morgan shivered.

"Wait a minute," Doc Pete said. "I am also here as a volunteer." Then he blushed which made his blond hair seem even brighter.

Morgan held up her hands. "Stop it! All of you! You're only here as volunteer *deputies*. Not volunteer kissers." She paused. "Or whatever the word is."

"Nice try, fellas. But I can't win unless it's Caleb," Mr. Dominic said. He sighed and hung his head. "And he's too stuffy."

"Now look here—" Cal began.

"Okay guys." JJ interrupted. He waved in the trio of deputies. "Come on back to the kitchen. Have a cup of coffee and a cupcake. We'll discuss what your schedule is going to be for the next couple of days as well as your availability."

Beau opened his mouth to speak. JJ cut him off. "None of it involves kissing the captain."

He shrugged. "A guy can hope."

Morgan shook off the conversation. The kissing stuff was just too weird. Not that she hadn't randomly felt a tingle when Cal looked at her a certain way, but there was no going down that particular path at least until Ian's murder was solved. She owed her husband that much. Morgan shifted her focus on the Maine Coon instead and stroked the cat's back. "What do you know about Tarot cards," she asked Cal, keeping her eyes on Griselda.

"I know their origins are in the Italian card game, *Tarocchi*. Late fourteenth, early fifteenth century. They evolved into fortune telling implements in the late eighteenth century." He offered Gris another treat. "Why ask me when you have a passel of psychics over at the bookstore you can get info from?" He considered that. "Passel? Huh. What exactly does one call a group of psychics?"

"No clue. That's your department. And it's because you have a head full of random knowledge that I'm asking you first. Consider it supplemental research."

"Any card in particular?"

Morgan retrieved the card found in Rocky's hand from the evidence box and placed it on the counter between them.

"Ah, The Fool," Cal said. He carefully picked up the plastic bag and considered the design on the back and front. "Traditional Rider-Waite deck. Surprising, really, if it's actually his card. Most younger readers use more modern decks at this point in time." He put it back down. "Interesting choice."

"Rocky grabbed a deck out of Edna's van last night. Maybe this is from that deck. He said she'd promised him one of hers," Morgan said. "What do you think of the meaning?"

Cal raised an eyebrow. "Morgan, I can't imagine you haven't already explored all of this."

"I have but, like I said, supplemental research." She blew out a breath. "The way you see the world is different than how I see it. As much as I hate to admit it—and you know I do—your view can be helpful once in a while."

"Better than not at all." He smiled. "Okay. So, The Fool symbolizes many things. On the surface, one given to folly, a true fool. Go deeper, though, and this card is about completion, taking chances, shrugging off the weight of the world and stepping into your true self."

"I wonder which one of those messages the killer was trying to send. Rocky did say he was ready to step fully into his role as psychic at the Perch Mouth Thursday night."

"My opinion? Given that the word *fraud* was discovered on or around each of the victims, I'd lean more toward the obvious meaning. To fool someone is to deceive them."

"And a fraud would be a deceiver." Morgan rolled the thought through her mind.

Cal rubbed his chin. "Maybe the killer thought the psychic was real and he or she changed their mind during the reading. Feeling deceived they killed the psychic and then left a calling card so to speak. It might be worth having this conversation with Jack or Starman, get their take on the card's meaning." He checked his watch. "The fair has another couple of hours to go. They're probably still there."

"Jack gives me a headache. I'll start with Starman."

CHAPTER 10

MORGAN LEFT the station and sat in her truck for a few moments. Organizing her thoughts and questions for Jack and Starman, she watched life in Bijoux go on around her. The end of season tourists wandered the streets with their bags of souvenirs. Several teenagers in wetsuits carried paddle boards, heading toward the beach at the end of Main Street straight ahead. Tut waved from across the way as he rolled out a vintage enduro style Yammie he was restoring. Life in Bijoux went on, in spite of the two recent murders. Humans were either amazingly resilient or blissfully unaware. Perhaps most people lived life somewhere in the middle. With a sigh, she started the truck and pulled away from the curb.

"DUDE, you're such a hack. Go find your own clients," Morgan heard Starman say as she entered the Raven's Nest courtyard. He was, of course, talking to Jack. She glanced around. None of the readers were paying attention to them, though a few locals and tourists looked a bit uncomfortable.

"You, sir, are no better than those charlatans who tell old lonely people they'll find love and be young and beautiful again." Jack crossed his arms across his wide chest. "And I happen to know you've done exactly that."

Starman waved a hand. "You're insane, man. Always have been."

"Well, that's the pot calling the kettle."

"Do you two go on like this all the time?" Morgan asked as she approached the pair.

"Only when we're together," Starman said.

"You might want to rethink that answer. I've seen both of your social media posts."

Jack and Starman turned in unison toward Morgan. "What are you doing tracking us on social media?" Jack asked.

"So not cool," Starman added.

"Investigating two murders, remember?"

"We're not suspects."

"Everyone is a suspect until cleared," Cal added from behind Morgan. "That's our good captain's credo."

Morgan frowned. "It's not 'my credo,' it's good investigative policy."

He flung an arm around her shoulder. "And you take it to the nth degree."

She shot him a look.

He dropped his arm and held up his hands. "Not that there's anything wrong with that. How can we help you?"

"Starman, a word in private, please?"

Starman narrowed his eyes. "How private? Last time you had a private conversation with someone they ended up dead. I'm not looking to shed my earthly form anytime soon, you get me?" He looked her up and down. "Especially considering you might be the killer. That news reporter makes a good case for it, you know. So does my son."

Morgan made a mental note to have another conversation with Connie. Not that it would probably do any good, but the woman needed to stop broadcasting crazy assumptions. It was unprofessional not to mention slanderous. She'd follow up with Rob later, too. She huffed. "I can assure you I'm not a killer."

"Though she is especially irritable and angry right now," Cal interjected. "Given the murders and the fact that she's pondering dating again."

"What are you, the peanut gallery? And I'm not planning on dating anyone anytime in the foreseeable future," Morgan said, exasperated.

"I can give you a prediction about that," Starman said. He straightened and continued, "I can help you understand your personal anger dynamics so much better through the use of Psychic Astrology."

"Oh, please," Jack said. "There's no such thing as Psychic Astrology. You made that up." He looked at Morgan. "If you want a true and accurate reading, I am at your service."

"No. No readings. Ever. Geez," Morgan said. Her phone pinged. The message was from JJ. *I have the release from Mayor Ed and a match on the print.* He included a screenshot of the juvenile record. Morgan sighed. "Raincheck on that talk, Starman. Jack, I'll need you to come down to the station with me. I have some questions for you, and it'll be more comfortable to talk there."

"Not to mention the deputy is probably there. She won't be able to kill you with a witness around," Starman added.

Jack stared hard at Morgan. "You think I did it. You think I killed Edna and Rocky. Maybe even those others."

"That's ridiculous!" Starman shouted. "I've known this guy for most of my adult life. He is not capable of murder."

"What, now you're best friends?" Morgan asked. "Come on, Jack. Let's go."

"What's this really all about?" Cal asked.

Before Morgan could reply, Jack said, "Like I said, Morgan thinks I killed all those poor psychics."

"I didn't say that."

"You didn't have to. You forget my line of work."

"Well, that seems ludicrous," Cal said. He looked at Jack. "I've never gotten a psycho-killer vibe from this guy."

"Oh, and you've been around a lot of murderers, have you?" The words were out of Morgan's mouth before she really thought about them. She watched the color drain from Cal's face. Dammit. It had only been a few months since he'd been held at gunpoint on the beach, his life threatened. Or, more specifically, the life of his gothic romance writing persona of Josie Steele. "Look, Cal—" Morgan began.

He held up his hand. "Save it." He turned and walked away.

BACK AT THE POLICE STATION, Morgan motioned to the guest chair across from her desk. "Have a seat." Jack Steve obliged, shifting until

he was comfortable. JJ perched on the corner of Morgan's desk, his arms crossed tight against his chest.

"Why do it?" JJ asked. "What do you have against your own kind?"

Jack sighed, but only stared straight ahead, not answering.

"Maybe they had information on him he didn't want out and this was his revenge," Morgan offered.

Jack shifted in the chair, but still didn't speak.

"Nah," JJ said. "I think he was taking out the competition."

"Oh for god's sake," Jack boomed. "You two sound like a couple of annoying magpies."

Morgan raised an eyebrow wondering, once again, if the man had a volume control. "Magpies who hold your fate in their hands, so you might want to play nice and cooperate."

Jack leaned back in the chair, rubbed his eyes, and ran his hands through his thick silver hair. "You have it all wrong. *All* wrong."

"Enlighten us," JJ said. He grabbed his desk chair and wheeled it over, sat down and faced Jack, one knee almost touching the older man's.

"If that's meant to intimidate, it won't work," Jack said, though he did angle himself slightly away from JJ.

"Jack, we have your print on the card found in Rocky's hand," Morgan said.

"How would you get my fingerprints without my permission?"

"Juvenile record."

"Impossible. That record was sealed. My father's lawyer specifically set it up to prevent casual access." Jack considered the information for a moment. "It should have been expunged by now, anyway. That was almost fifty years ago."

"You have to request a record be removed," Morgan explained. "And, apparently, neither your father nor his lawyer ever followed up. So, tell us your story, Jack Steve," Morgan said. "I know what's in the file, but I want to hear it from you."

Jack shook his head and took a deep breath. "I've lived a lot of years on this beautiful planet, and only got in trouble that one time. I was fifteen and looking to rebel against my family. Got in with a bad crowd. I was their lookout for a liquor store robbery. Up in Saint Ignace. They wanted to buy drugs. The robbery went south and they shot the night clerk. Before I knew it, the police arrived, and we were all arrested." He sighed. "My family had money earned from the timber industry up north. Dad was able to make the charges against me go away since I wasn't in the store when the murder happened. He said no one would ever know as long as I kept my nose clean. He held the record over my head, to make sure I held to the straight and narrow."

"You consider being a psychic as keeping to the 'straight and narrow?'" Morgan asked.

Jack bristled. "I don't *call* myself anything. I am what I am. Always have been."

"Then why kill your kindred spirits?" JJ asked.

"Again, I didn't kill them. I didn't even know any of them. Well, except for Edna. Rocky I only knew peripherally through her." He looked at the officers. "I knew something bad was going to happen that night, when I was a kid, and I ignored my gut. I promised myself I'd never do that again."

Morgan dangled the evidence bag with The Fool tarot card in front of her. "Can you explain to me, then, why your print is on this card?"

He leaned forward and studied the card. "I'm going to take my personal tarot deck out of my pocket, okay?" Jack reached into the back pocket of his jeans and pulled out a small black silk bag with a red tie around it. He opened the bag and fanned the deck out on Morgan's desk, face up. "The Fool is missing. That card is from my deck."

Morgan picked up one of the cards and studied it, comparing it to the one in the evidence bag. Same blue tartan design on the back, same artistic style, similar wear around the edges. She put both cards down and folded her hands. "That only makes you look more guilty."

"Do you think I don't know that?" Pausing, he ran his fingers over his moustache. "I don't usually do readings; I keep these cards for my own use. I was in the local bar — Perch Mouth? — yesterday and thought it would be fun for a change. You can ask the bartender. I read for her."

"How many other people did you read for?"

"Maybe half a dozen or so. Look, I wasn't keeping count. Someone obviously palmed this card to frame me."

"Why would someone want to do that?"

He held out his hands. "I've solved a lot of crimes. Maybe your killer is worried I'll do the same here and expose them."

"Morgan, what's going on?" Zoe asked as she walked into the station.

Morgan stood. "We're working. Did you need something?"

"Yes. I need my friend. Jack's graciously offered to perform the wedding ceremony for us on Monday and I want to go over our vows."

"I'm sorry, Zoe. But we're conducting an investigation here."

"Oh, for heaven's sake." Zoe brushed past the front counter and stood next to Jack. "I've known this man for most of this lifetime, not to mention all the others. He's not a murderer."

Jack threw up his hands. "That's what I've been telling them. I'm positive I was heading for the airport when Edna was killed," Jack offered. "As far as Rocky goes, I'm fairly certain I was speaking in front of the crowd at Cal's when he was murdered."

Morgan had forgotten that point. He was right, he *was* giving the talk when Rocky was killed. She was there. *Dammit.* She sat back down.

Griselda wandered over to Jack and threaded herself through his legs. He went still. "Edna. She's here." He looked Morgan straight in the eye. "You already know the killer. The clue is in the animal."

"Griselda?" Morgan asked.

"I don't know." Jack shook his head. "That's all she said. She's gone now."

Morgan rolled her neck. "Why is it, if you're a psychic, you can't just come straight out and say what you mean? Why all the subterfuge and obtuse clues?"

"Morgan," Zoe said. Morgan turned to her soon-to-be stepmom. "That's just not how it works with a lot of us, especially the empaths. We get images and impressions and feelings and words. It's up to the person we're giving the information to, to figure out what it means *for them.*" She placed a hand on Jack's shoulder. "Now, may I take my friend with me?"

Morgan glanced at JJ. He looked as disturbed as she felt at the moment. She waved a hand. "Fine. Fine. You can go, Jack. Just don't leave Bijoux for the time being."

He set his mouth in a firm line. "You can rest assured, I'm not going anywhere until *we* solve this case."

She could only stare after him as they left. Why did everyone insist on getting involved? JJ handed her a bottle of aspirin and a glass of water. "Thanks," she said. "Back to square one." She popped two aspirin and chased it down with the water. "I'm going to run over to Dave's and grab some food. You want anything?"

JJ looked at his watch. "Nah, thanks anyway. It's almost four. I'm supposed to meet Hannah over at the Raven's Nest for a couples reading in a few."

Morgan raised an eyebrow. "Really?"

"Really." He shrugged. "The things we do for love, right?"

CHAPTER 17

"CAPTAIN MORGAN! HOW ARE YOU DOING?" Jerome made his way around the counter at Dave's Deli and looped his arm through hers as he led her to a booth.

Morgan glanced down at the contact and then met Jerome's eyes. "What's going on?"

"I'm sure you have enough on your mind and I just don't want you disturbed while you eat." He glanced up at the television mounted high on the wall, over the back of a booth.

The sound was off, but the text ticker was running beneath the image of Connie Graham reporting on the latest murder. She caught the words "Detroit Killer" and "Is our Police Captain a cold-blooded and vicious murderer?" before Jerome spun her around, away from the set. "You sit here and ignore her vicious critique of you and your work. I'm sure you're doing everything you can to solve this case and not killing anyone." He pulled a pad and pencil out of his white server's apron. "What will you have?"

Morgan sighed. Jerome was right. She wasn't going to let Connie ruin her meal. "Patty melt, fries, Diet Coke, please." She smiled up at Jerome. "Thanks."

"Anything for you." He winked and left to put in the order.

She caught a movement out of the corner of her eye. Cal, dropping onto a stool at the counter. "Really?" she said.

He spun on the stool to face Morgan. "Really."

She rolled her eyes and patted the table. "I'm sure I'll regret this but come on. Join me."

Cal waited a beat, then got up and slid into the seat across from her in the booth.

"Still pouting?"

"Men don't pout. We brood."

"Still brooding?"

He adjusted his glasses and leaned back in the seat, crossing his arms against his chest. "That I am."

"Oh, for heaven's sake, Cal. I said I didn't mean it. Let it go." She met his eyes when he didn't respond. They were cold and hard and she could imagine this exact glare silencing an entire lecture hall of chatty university students. She reached across the table and touched his arm. "I'm sorry. I was insensitive to your situation," she added and drew back. "Does that help?"

Cal continued to look at her as Jerome dropped off Morgan's Diet Coke, his standard iced tea, and took his order of a BLT and chips. "You really are not good at apologies, are you? I suppose that's the best I'm going to get so yeah, okay, you're forgiven." He relaxed and propped his arms on the table. "So where are you on this case? What happened with Jack?"

"Jack looks suspicious, but it also looks like he's going to alibi out. We're almost nowhere." Morgan shook her head. "After Rocky's declaration of how happy he was to be shed of Edna the other night at the Perch Mouth, I figured him for a suspect."

"And now that he's dead, it probably wasn't him." He unfolded his napkin and placed it across his lap. "Unless you're thinking he did it and someone else killed him? Are you considering the possibility of a serial killer? Because it's certainly starting to feel like that."

She glanced around the deli. Too late for lunch and a little too early for dinner, so it wasn't crowded. Still, she leaned forward and whispered, "Look, I'm not discounting the possibility, but it's nothing I want to discuss publicly. It's bad enough Connie is spouting her Detroit Killer theories all over TV again."

"Not to mention her 'Captain Morgan as the killer' story."

Morgan stabbed a straw into her pop. "I may turn murderer just to put her out of my misery."

Cal laughed. "That I understand." He shook out a packet of organic sugar into his iced tea and took a drink. "And believe me, the psychics are riled up enough without adding a serial killer vibration into their already itchy mix."

"Vibration? Who are you?" Morgan shook her head and smiled.

"Hey, what can I say? I'm good at picking up the lingo in groups of people. Who else are you considering? Besides Jack Steve, that is."

"Jack is on the low end of suspects at this point. Like I said, it looks like he's got an airtight alibi for these two murders. He was at the airport, boarding a plane, when Edna was killed. And giving his talk when Rocky was strangled." She took a drink of her pop. "Do you know anything about Starman's son, Rob?"

"Only what he said earlier. Never met him before, but he sure seems unhappy with his dad's chosen line of work."

"That he does. What do you know about Davey Rocket and Daisy?"

"Are you serious?" Cal laughed. "Yeah, no. Those two are about as harmless as anyone you'd ever hope to meet."

"What I hear you saying is you've known them for a while and can attest to their character?"

He considered the question and shook his head. "No. I haven't known them long. It's just the impression I get from them. I suppose they could have done it as much as anyone at this point."

"What time is the closing dinner tomorrow night?" Morgan asked.

"The fair closes at four and we gather at six. Dinner is at seven."

"Then we have Dad and Zoe's wedding on Monday and the psychics will be dispersing after that. Not a lot of time."

"You mean if it's one of them." He considered that. "What are the odds?"

"I don't know. As good as any, at this point."

Jerome brought their food. "Anything else, folks?"

Cal smiled. "We're good for now, thanks."

Morgan poured some ketchup onto her plate and ate a couple of fries. She was getting nowhere fast. She pulled out her phone and texted JJ, asking him to look into Davey and Daisy. "I need a ride to clear my head. There has to be something I'm missing. Maybe I'll head out to the Preserve, look over the area where Edna was camped again, check out Rocky's vehicle."

"Did I ever tell you I used to ride? It's how I got around in grad school. Had a nifty powder blue Vespa. Matching helmet, too. I was a hell raiser on that thing."

Morgan gaped at him.

"What? Do I have something on my face?" he dabbed at his mouth with his napkin. "Did I get it?"

"I'm looking at you because a Vespa is a *scooter*. It is *not* the same as riding an actual motorcycle. Holy crap." She took a bite of her sandwich. "There is absolutely no way to raise hell on a scooter. It goes against all the laws of two-wheeled motorized riding."

"I should've known." Cal rolled his eyes. "You're a bike snob."

"That I am." She looked out the window. An early morning ride would be the thing, when no one was out and about and she could actually think without interruption. Not to mention she could use a little down time this evening to unwind and see where her mind went with the case. "I need to grab Gris from the station and get her home, so I'm thinking a morning ride."

"You said 'home,'" Cal observed.

"Yeah, so?"

"You said you needed to get Gris and take her home." He grinned. "I see your soft spot showing. You're going to keep her, aren't you?"

She had been trying hard to not think that far ahead on the outside chance a relative of Edna's showed up and claimed her. But she and the cat *were* bonding...so, maybe...? "I suppose if no one claims her?"

"No one is going to claim that mini black mountain lion." Cal laughed. "Plus, she's already adopted you. I don't think you have a choice."

"I'll want to wait until the investigation is over before officially taking her in." She smiled. "But yeah. She's mine now, isn't she?"

Cal smiled. "That she is."

"So, want to ride out with me to the Preserve in the morning? I'll show you what it's like to be on an actual motorcycle." She winked. "You will, of course, be riding on the back."

THE NEXT MORNING, Morgan was up at six a.m. and texted Cal to make sure he was up and getting ready to go. She poured herself a cup of freshly brewed coffee and sat with Gris beside her on the front porch, enjoying the peacefulness of the morning. After grabbing a shower, she dressed in jeans and a long-sleeved flannel shirt. It was always cold riding in the morning. She grabbed her extra helmet and strapped it to the back of the Bonnie's flat seat with bungee cords, then shrugged on her heavy black leather riding jacket. After snapping her helmet on and pulling on a pair of gloves, she mounted the bike and fired up the engine. Honestly, there was nothing like the sound of an old airhead. She smiled and rode away from her cottage, heading toward Main Street.

She pulled up in front of the Raven's Nest bookstore twenty minutes later and waited for Cal. There he was, in the back, closing the gate. Morgan hit the kill switch, kicked the side stand down and dismounted. "Here, this should fit you pretty good," she said to Cal as she handed him the helmet. He pulled it on, fastened the buckle, and gave her a thumbs up.

Morgan's chest clenched. The helmet had been Ian's. He and Cal were about the same build, so she wasn't surprised it fit him, but she was surprised how she felt seeing it on someone again. She shook off the nostalgia, smiled, and got back on her bike. "Whatever you do, keep your feet up on the passenger pegs. Leave them there until we get to where we're going, parked, and the bike turned off." She turned the key in the ignition and revved the engine.

"Please," Cal shouted over the rumble as he climbed on the back of the bike. "I told you, I used to ride. I know the rules."

With that, Morgan pulled away from the curb. The bike jerked slightly when she hit the throttle and Cal teetered before grabbing her around the waist. She tamped down all the feels threatening to over-load her—the helmet, the way he held on, their easy friendship—and focused on heading out of Bijoux, toward Lac Voo Nature Preserve.

It was still early enough that the two-lane highway was clear of the usual beach traffic, especially with it being the end of tourist season Up North. Morgan turned onto the asphalt drive leading into the preserve, only to find the parking lot filled with cars and bicycles. Curious, she turned the engine off, engaged the side stand, and dismounted. She nodded at Cal and he did the same. Helmets and gear off and hanging on the bike, they stood side by side and took in the sight before them.

It looked like most of the psychics were here and hanging around the edge of the campground, about thirty feet from the water. Miranda, the climate-activist teen, and her crew were standing on the beach, looking out over the horizon. She'd heard they were on watch for another Messie appearance.

Where the psychics stood, votive candles were lit and placed inside a large white circle drawn on top of the sand. Rennie was off to the side, blowing and fanning some smoke coming out of a large shell with a feather. "What do you suppose they're doing?" Morgan asked.

"From the looks of it, they've cast a circle for a ceremony and Rennie's burning sage to clear any negativity from the area."

Morgan shook her head. "You really are a font of random information."

He shrugged. "You asked."

Zoe waved and motioned for the pair to join her at the outer edge of the circle. She hugged them both and stopped Morgan when she started to cross the white outline. "The circle is cast. None may enter who are not already there." She pointed to where Janine the All Knowing, Sven the Seer, and Starman the Whatever were standing in the center, back to back, eyes closed. Holding tapered candles, the psychics gathered around the perimeter and started chanting 'Ommmmmmmm."

Morgan took a step back. This was all crazy. She'd go talk to the teens on the beach. At least their brand of crazy she understood. Well, mostly.

"Wait," Cal said. "Maybe something will come up."

"I'm not here for predictions."

Cal blew out a breath. "You know better than most that clues can come from unexpected places. Why not see what happens?"

"Fine, fine." Morgan squeezed back into the outer circle between Zoe and Cal. She scanned the area. From the looks of it, all thirty-three of the attendees were here. "What's this about?" she whispered to Zoe.

"We're having a vigil for Edna and Rocky. Their spirits have been hanging around and our fear is their souls will get trapped on the earth plane. We want to help send them on their way."

"Edna!" Starman shouted from the center, his eyes still closed. "I feel your presence. What messages do you have for us before you pierce the eternal veil once and for all? Or, at least, until the journey into your next lifetime?"

"Rocky!" Sven shouted. "I feel you as well. What words do you carry from the other realms?"

Janine dropped to her knees, sobbing. "So much pain. So much fear. So much left to do."

"Is she going to be okay?" Morgan asked Zoe.

"Yes, she's channeling a message. Give her a minute," Zoe whispered.

"The animal. It's the blue animal," Janine cried. "So strong, so damaged. Unloved." She hugged her arms around her and wiped away the tears. When she opened her eyes, she met Morgan's and pointed at the police captain. "You! Do something before the animal strikes again. Their life mission is incomplete, they threaten all of us. You must act!"

All eyes on her, Morgan squared her shoulders. "What are you talking about? Are you suggesting we have an animal in Bijoux killing people?"

"Could be a werewolf," Cal whispered. Zoe shot him a glare and he quit talking.

"Hey!" Miranda shouted from the beach. "Look!" Everyone turned to where she was pointing. A large, dark green, humped blob was floating just above the surface of the water. "Messie is here!"

Morgan and Cal hurried to the edge of the water, about half the psychics following close behind. The others stayed close to the circle. "Well, that's something," Cal said.

"You believe in sea monsters, don't you?" Morgan asked.

"Whether or not I believe is not the question. The only question is, what is that?" he said, pointing to the moving entity.

"A lake sturgeon? They can get up to three hundred pounds. The conventional thinking is Messie is just a big old fish no one's been able to catch."

"It's not a sturgeon," Zoe said. "It's a sign from Edna and Rocky." She turned to Morgan and her eyes were closed. "Messie is elusive, as is the animal. In our midst, yet unseen."

"Zoe," Morgan said.

Zoe opened her eyes and took one of Morgan's hands and one of Cal's in each of hers. "You will solve this mystery. Together."

As Zoe finished speaking, Messie dove under the water and everyone cheered. A long thin tale, maybe fifteen feet long, pointed straight up in the air before it, too, vanished. "Not a lake sturgeon," Cal whispered. "Not by a long shot."

CHAPTER 18

"WHAT ARE YOU DOING?" Morgan asked as she approached a small, older SUV. Jack Steve spun around.

"Nothing." His eyes shot back and forth between the officer and Cal. He patted the roof of the vehicle. "Nothing at all."

Morgan held her hand out.

"What?"

She wiggled her fingers until Jack reluctantly deposited a small lock picking kit onto her palm. He kicked at the sand while she examined it. Not fancy, cheaply made, and barely usable. "You said yesterday you'd given up your early life of crime. This says otherwise. Reputable folks do not carry around lock picking kits." She held up the small vinyl case. "Where did you get this? The back of a comic book?"

Jack straightened. "If you must know, yes. That's exactly where I got it."

"Did you get the x-ray glasses too?" Cal asked. "I could never get my pair to work."

Morgan stared at him. "You should probably stop talking now. You're only adding to your professor weirdness persona." She looked back at Jack. "Explain yourself, please."

"This is Rocky's vehicle. I had a hunch. Not a premonition or anything like that, just a good old-fashioned hunch." He shook his head. "It was like a breath of fresh air, really, to have an original thought not tainted by guides and spirits." He glanced at Cal and frowned. "Never got my x-ray glasses to work either. I had dreams of seeing through walls."

"I bet that's what you dreamed of seeing through." Morgan rolled her eyes, then scolded herself. How had she not thought to look for

Rocky's car? *Damn* "Now, back to the real conversation. Why are you here?"

"In the spirit of full disclosure, and to further cement our professional relationship, I will tell you everything I know."

"We don't have a professional relationship but go ahead anyway."

"I remembered hearing someone was looking for Rocky yesterday, for a reading. I thought Rocky might have had an appointment book with names in it," Jack offered. "Nothing more nefarious than that."

Damn. I should've thought of that, Morgan admitted to herself. "So, did you find one?"

Jack gave Morgan the once over. "If you would embrace your witch-self, you'd already know the answer and wouldn't have to ask. But since you continue to be in denial, no, I found nothing." He looked at Cal. "It's a shame, really. Power exudes from this one and she fears it."

Cal peeked at Morgan out of the corner of his eye. Her jaw was clenched. "Sorry, Jack. The only thing she fears right now is smacking you and getting charged with police brutality."

Morgan stuffed the small kit into her back pocket. Jack started to protest. "I'm keeping this. You can return to your friends over there. Stay out of police business or we'll need to have another talk down at the station again, only this time there'll be bars between us."

Jack huffed. "Well, I never."

"And you shouldn't." Morgan nodded toward the psychics. "Looks like they're waiting for you."

"Yes, yes, of course they are. I'm somewhat of a leader for them, you know. They'll need my help closing the circle and putting Edna and Rocky to rest." He walked away, but added over his shoulder, "Not that they'll get any rest while the murderer is still on the loose."

"I can't believe I forgot about checking Rocky's vehicle," Morgan said to Cal.

"Cut yourself some slack. There's a lot going on."

"Yeah, but this is my job. I'm not allowed to make these sorts of mistakes." Morgan sighed. Self-recrimination wouldn't get her anywhere. She opened the car door and gave Rocky's vehicle a thorough going over, but nothing interesting turned up. Unless you counted his collection of shawls, turbans, and unopened packages of bubble gum. Beyond that, there was nothing to help figure out who killed him. Her phone pinged and she checked the message. "Doc Pete has the DNA results from Griselda's claws. He's going to meet me at the station. C'mon, I'll drop you off."

Cal looked at her, eyebrows raised.

"I'm taking you back to the Raven's Nest, not the station, in case you're wondering. Don't you have a psychic fair to get ready for?"

"That's not for another hour, plus I have Billy taking care of whatever the psychics might need this morning. Which is good because I'd rather not miss seeing the Doc around you. I'm sure you noticed how he turns an interesting shade of red."

"I don't exist for your entertainment, you know. I have two murders to solve and you insist on being in the way." Morgan pushed her choppy bangs out of her eyes. When this case was done, a haircut was first on the agenda.

He punched her gently on the arm and grinned. "Now who's acting all stuffy?"

MORGAN GAVE UP. If she dropped Cal at the store, he would only walk over. Might as well save the gas. She pulled up in front of the station and, true to his word, Doc Pete was waiting, perched on the wood bench outside the entrance. She waved to him as she unlocked the door. "Come in, please."

She angled around the counter and both Cal and Pete stood on the other side. Cal leaned sideways, his elbow on the counter, and looked at Pete. "What do you have for us?"

"There is no us," Morgan said. As the words were coming out of her mouth, she wondered why she even bothered to say anything at all. *Damn he was stubborn.*

"Should he be here? Isn't this private police business between an officer and a doctor?" Doc Pete asked. He looked at Cal out of the corner of his eye, then back at Morgan. "Isn't he potentially a security risk to your investigation?"

Morgan shook her head. "He's always a risk. I find it's best to ignore him," she said. "He eventually gets the hint and wanders off."

"Well, okay." Doc Pete pulled an envelope out of his back pocket and retrieved the contents. "Here are the results of the DNA testing from the blood I found on Griselda's claws." He paused. "Do you know we share about ninety percent of our DNA with cats? It's just that little ten percent that makes them kitties and not humans. Or, I suppose, us human and them kitties. All their soft fur, innate cuteness, and bad attitude exists just within that small ten percent. Isn't that fascinating?"

"Sure....?" Morgan said. If she'd entertained even a smidgen of a possibility of going out with him, Pete just shut that down with his kitty comments. "But what can you tell me about the test?"

"Oh. Oh, yes. I found two different DNA strands and compared what I had with what Wood's been able to gather. One strand matched Edna. The other is unidentified."

"What does that mean?" Cal asked.

"Well, it's more human than cat, sort of a human/animal hybrid."

"That seems odd," Morgan said. Janine's words came to mind, *Do something before the animal strikes again*, and she shook off the foreboding.

"A little," Pete said. "But I believe it was likely the human DNA was contaminated with Griselda's. Because of the contamination, there's no way to get a conclusive human match."

"Makes more sense than something like a werewolf — werecat? — walking among us," Cal said. "Though Griselda is pretty big."

"Wouldn't that be something," Pete said, his eyes wide. "Michigan does have its fair share of cryptids, you know, besides Messie. Some even with werewolf characteristics, like the Dog Man."

"The French called it *Loup Garou*. The legend in Michigan goes all the way back to the 1700s and the *voyageurs*," Cal added. "Native cultures have similar folklore about a half wolf/half man who roamed the woods at night as well."

The two men stared off in the distance, as if imagining such a creature walking down Main Street. Morgan cleared her throat. "Why don't you two take this fascinating discussion outside?" Morgan held her hand out to the Doc. "I'll take the results. Thank you for bringing them over." She smiled at him. "I appreciate your help and everything you've done for Griselda."

He stared at her like the proverbial deer in the headlights. The blush started at the base of his neck and flushed its way up to the top of his head, making his blonde hair and blue eyes glow in bold relief.

Morgan noticed Cal was watching the color change with an intense fascination. She shoved at his shoulder. "Go. Go away. Both of you. I have work to do."

"But it's Sunday," Pete said. "Maybe you should get some lunch first? With me?"

Morgan froze, which she considered must be some sort of Cro-Magnon self-preservation tactic still locked in her genetic makeup. Who knew? She'd stared down hardened criminals and never gave it a second thought, always acted with quick reflexes.

Cal laid an arm across the shorter man's shoulders and steered him toward the door. "C'mon, Pete. I have a little time before I have to be at the fair. Cap'n is busy chasing criminals. I'll grab some food with you."

"Um, okay."

Cal tossed Morgan a look over his shoulder as he and Doc Pete left. "You owe me," he mouthed.

Morgan could not disagree. She crossed her arms on the counter and laid her head down, eyes closed. Where was the quiet lakeside town of her childhood where the worst thing could happen was a beach streaker or pot-smoking teens on the preserve?

When she moved back, three months ago, she'd noted the physical changes in Bijoux—the trendy shops and coffee houses—and wondered if they reflected deeper shifts to what had been a more simple way of life in the tourist town. But maybe seeing through the lens of her childhood wasn't a good way to look at something. Her years in Detroit and Ian's murder had definitely made her cynical, which probably wasn't a good way to see the world either. Even Able, had mellowed out over the years. Balance. She needed balance. Maybe it wasn't enough to hop on her bike and go for a ride. Maybe she needed to embrace change like everyone else around her had done. Maybe yoga classes would do the trick. Yoga was supposed to be good for such things, or so she'd heard from Frankie. And Liz. They both attended classes several times a week. And there *was* a new studio in town.

Voices outside drew her attention and Morgan raised her head. A line was forming at Hal's. Must be another unscheduled Coffee Cake Day. *Cake made everything better.* She locked the station door behind her and walked over to see her dad.

Morgan reached the front of the line and started to open the exit door when someone yelled, "Cutter!"

Another joined in. "Line cutter there!"

Morgan turned around. "For heaven's sake. We've been through this before. I am not cutting the line. I'm going to talk to my dad."

"Oh, Morgan," Mr. Dominic began, "you know you have to obey the rules of Coffee Cake Day just like anyone else." He gave her the once over. "Kissed that fancy professor of yours yet?"

"What? No! He's not 'my professor' and I'm not having this conversation."

"I understand. You need some coffee cake to sweeten him up, get him to like you enough to plant one on."

"I do not need coffee cake to get someone to kiss me."

"Can't hurt, though," Cal said from behind her.

Morgan turned. "Why are you always lurking? I thought you were getting food with Pete."

"He had an emergency and had to run to the clinic."

"Well, go keep an eye on your psychics," she said to Cal. Then, to Mr. Dominic, "And you. Stop placing bets on me."

Mr. Dominic hung his head. "Now the captain won't let me wager money on kissing." Several people standing around him, patted his back and shot dirty looks at Morgan.

"How am I the bad guy here?"

"Don't make her mad, Mr. Dominic," Connie warned walking up to them. "Or you might end up her next victim."

Morgan took a step toward Connie. Cal put a hand on her arm and whispered, "Let's go get some of that coffee cake."

She allowed herself to be led inside, chants of 'cutters' and 'killer' ringing out behind her. "I am really getting tired of her antics," Morgan muttered.

"Hey, Morgan!" Able called out. "Come on back. Fresh coffee and a new coffee cake recipe today — lemon poppy seed."

"What's the occasion?" she asked. "You're off calendar again."

"Celebrating in advance of tomorrow's ceremony." Able smiled and handed them two steaming mugs. "Just what the doctor ordered."

"And here's the other half of the prescription," Zoe said, handing them each a napkin with a large piece of cake.

Morgan smiled her thanks as Zoe turned back to the line of folks waiting for their slice.

"You're worried," Able said. "And those circles around your eyes tell me you're not sleeping. That's not a good combination for working a case, especially one as intense as this one."

Morgan sighed and stepped over to the side of the makeshift coffee bar, away from the crowd. Able followed. "Dad, you're lucky you never had to deal with death while you were on the job. And, you know, it's not that I can't handle it, but it's been a lot to manage in such a short amount of time."

"It doesn't help that Connie keeps dogging you, either," her father growled. "I have a mind to talk to the station manager about her behavior. That woman is beyond unprofessional. She's downright dangerous with her crazy theories."

"Thanks Dad, I can handle Connie. She's goading me into a confrontation so she can get it on camera. But I'm not going to give it to her."

Able gave Morgan's shoulders a comforting squeeze. "Any developments on the case?"

"Nothing substantial. Rocky was the main suspect. Since he's no longer viable, we're now investigating some of the other psychics."

"Why assume it's another psychic?"

"There are a lot of rivalries and Edna, the first victim, wasn't well-liked in the community. It stands to reason it could be one of them." She shook her head. "And then there's Starman's son, who thinks these people are all frauds." She leaned in and whispered. "Between us, that exact word turned up at each murder scene."

"I'd be more inclined to go down that road than the psychics. These are Zoe's friends. Some of them are like family to her." He glanced at his fiancée. "I hope for her sake it's not one of them."

Morgan sighed. "Her friends have been handing out predictions like crazy, too. Whether to divert attention from themselves or not, I have no idea. I can't believe I'm even giving it any thought, but they keep talking about an animal being the killer."

"Not just any animal," Cal said as he joined them. "A werewolf-cat hybrid."

Able eyed Cal. "What, you too? Stop floating ridiculous rumors like that. You know as well as I do how itchy everyone around here gets when people start talking about ghosts and monsters."

"It's not ridiculous. The *Loup Garou* is well known in Michigan." Cal took a bite of cake and pushed his glasses up. "Goes along with the territory of being the most haunted town on Lake Michigan."

Zoe joined the conversation. "Ghosts and werewolves are two entirely different entities. One's dead and the other, though altered, is still very much alive." The crowd behind them started grumbling. "Sorry everyone, we're out of cake!" she called out.

"At least the Killer Captain got hers," someone said from near the door. "Maybe she'll be happy now and not kill anymore."

"Oh, for Pete's sake," Able shouted. "Go on, all of you!" Then he grinned. "But, hey, thanks for coming by. Stop in next week for my wedding day discounts and specials."

Morgan shook her head and had to smile a little. This place was crazy, but it was home.

"Well, I've heard enough. I'm heading over to the psychic fair." She glanced at her phone. "Some info from JJ on Davey and Daisy just popped into my email." She glanced at Cal. "I suppose you're coming?"

"Wouldn't miss it. Plus, I need to do some research on blue animals crossed with werewolves."

"And don't forget Messie," Zoe said. "She's tied into this somehow, too. It may be nothing more than Edna and Rocky sending messages through her, but you never know."

CHAPTER 19

"ALL OF YOU. Go back to your tables. This sort of public disturbance is not welcome in Bijoux and will not be tolerated!"

Morgan entered the psychic fair and found the readers divided into factions. The locals and tourists who were waiting for readings standing behind them and Beau Cornet was directing 'traffic.' "What's going on?" Morgan asked. "And what are you doing?"

"I was getting a palm reading from Janine over there," Beau said. "Someone said Edna's spirit was walking through the fair and another shouted out Rocky's name and said he was here, too. The next thing I knew, they were drawing up sides and arguing with each other." Beau glanced at his hand. "I didn't know I had that kind of power in my palm."

"And you thought you should do something about it?"

"Well, I am a volunteer deputy, so I exercised my deputy rights and tried to create order, which, honestly, I thought you'd appreciate." He grinned broadly. "It's why they're in lines now. Team Edna and Team Rocky. At least that's what they're calling themselves."

Jimmy the Groupie waved at Morgan from Team Rocky. She noticed he was wearing a glittery shawl, similar to the one Rocky wore.

"What's with the third group over there?"

"Oh, we're Team Animal." Janine said. "We believe the prophecies this week that an animal-human hybrid is the killer and Messie is somehow involved, possibly passing along secret messages telepathically to the murderer. Maybe even controlling the animal. We're cheering for them."

"You're cheering for a killer...?" Morgan rubbed her eyes and groaned. "Okay then. Who started all this?" No one replied, but Starman and Jack refused to meet her gaze. "You two again?"

"Edna is having a hard time being dead," Jack said. "And Rocky has no empathy for her whatsoever."

"Because Rocky is dead too!" Starman said. "Geez."

"Why do I keep finding you guys in the center of these disturbances? C'mon, let's go inside and talk. As for the rest of you—there are only a few more hours until this event is finished. Please try to keep the peace, okay?"

"You heard Morgan. Go on, back to your tables," Beau ordered. He flashed Morgan another grin. When she didn't return the gesture, he heaved a deep sigh and wandered back to Janine's table. "The way she acts, it's like she barely knows me," he complained. "And yet, we were in love once."

"It's been twenty years. It was high school. Let it go," Morgan shot over her shoulder as she led the two men into the Raven's Nest.

The room where Rocky's body had been found was still secured, so Morgan directed them to the back of the bookstore where a long table was set up for reading and research. She gestured to the library-style wooden chairs and sat opposite them. "I have the feeling you two know more than you're sharing. Start talking."

"There's a rumor—" Jack began.

"That psychics are being killed to cull their power," Starman finished.

"What the hell?" Morgan said. "That is *not* a thing..." She thought for a moment. *Suppose I've heard stranger theories.* "Is it?"

"It's been known to happen, but it's not something that ever makes the news. 'They' do a good job of keeping such things quiet, under the radar so to speak." Jack said the word *they* with air quotes.

"Who are 'they?'"

Starman's gaze scanned the room. Then he leaned forward and said in a whisper. "Dude. The Priesthood. They run everything." He sat back in his chair and crossed his arms. "I can't talk about it. I've already said too much."

Jack looked down his long nose at Starman. "You've always been overly paranoid. Besides, the Priesthood are not in Bijoux."

"You can't know that. All these psychics gathered in one spot? All this energy? We're just sitting ducks for them to pluck. Pluck, pluck, pluck."

As much as she hated the idea of conspiracy theories and under the radar groups, Morgan knew she had to follow every possible line of investigation. Humans were known to do horrendous things to each other, this much she did believe, had seen with her own eyes. "Back to the beginning, please," Morgan instructed. "What do you mean by culling power?"

"Well, yeah," Starman said. "There are people on the fringe who believe if you kill a psychic – a real one, mind you—their powers will enter you. The more you kill, the more powerful you become." He leaned forward and said sotto voce, "The Priesthood knows this, and they cover up the killing sprees to protect their own."

Morgan closed her eyes and breathed in and out. Okay, that was just plain crazy, and crazy she did not need.

"Did I hear mention of the Priesthood?" Cal asked as he pulled out a chair and sat next to Morgan. "Do you think they're somehow involved?"

"Tell me you don't believe in this shadow order, too?" Morgan said. "Seriously, Cal, I'm beginning to wonder about your brain."

He tapped his forehead "Lots of good information in here, just waiting to be accessed. I'm like a computer." He looked at the two men. "Now, back to the Priesthood."

Starman shoved at Jack. "Why do you have to talk so loud, man?"

Jack shoved back. "Why do you have to be such a pain in the ass?"

"Stop it or I'm locking you both up," Morgan ordered.

"On what charge?" Jack asked.

"Annoying the police captain."

"That's not a real thing," Starman countered. "I know my rights. I'll get my son to represent me."

"Yeah, you've been arrested multiple times, haven't you? And your son never helped. Let's talk about that." She pulled up an earlier text from JJ. "Public nuisance, disturbing the peace, drug possession. Are you moving up in the world? Looking to gain more power, as you call it?"

"It was pot, which is legal in a lot of states now. Besides, those old charges don't make me a murderer." He huffed. "Besides, I have enough power of my own, thank you very much."

"Right." Jack chuckled, then grew serious. "Are you looking into Davey Rocket and Daisy?"

"Premonition?" Morgan didn't need any more of those, either.

"Observation. They've been vocal about their campground issue with Edna. Still fussing about it today even, how Edna was trying to take over their host duties. Daisy seemed more miffed about it than Davey, though." Jack shrugged and stopped talking when Zoe and Rennie walked up.

"Morgan," they said in unison.

"Zoe, Rennie," Morgan greeted.

"Again?" Zoe asked and sighed, looking at the two men.

She stood and looked at the older women. "Yes. And I'll keep talking to them as long as I feel the need to."

"Oh, Morgan, it's not these two," Rennie said. "I mean, they're old fools to be sure, but not killers."

"Who are you calling old?' Starman asked.

"And fools?" Jack added.

Zoe frowned at the pair. "Both of you and you know it's true." She linked her arm with Rennie's. "We're beyond sick and tired of your ancient spat. We don't care that it's gone on for lifetimes. Finish it now or we're finished with the two of you."

Starman' eyes pleaded with Rennie. "My lady—.

She held up a hand and cut him off.

"What do you want us to do? Fight it out?" Starman frowned. "Dude has a good foot on me, you know."

Rennie sighed. "We want you to forgive each other and move on. Life is too short, especially as these last few days have taught us. But you both know that. Just admit it and be done with it."

Jack and Starman looked at each other out of the corner of their eyes. Jack, sighing, made the first move and held his hand out. Starman accepted it and they shook, then did a quick hug with a couple of hearty back slaps.

"Finally," Zoe said beaming. She turned to Morgan. "You have to understand they are incapable of doing such a vile thing as killing Edna and Rocky."

Morgan shrugged. "I appreciate these are your friends, but everyone's a suspect in a case like this."

"Until they're not," Cal added.

Morgan shot him a narrow-eyed look and continued, "Having said that, gentleman, you are free to go on about your day. I need some time to digest our conversation. We'll talk later if we need to." She watched them walk away, then turned to Cal, who dropped into the seat across the table from her. "Now, let's talk about *real* things, not werewolves or werecats or sea monsters or deep state conspiracies," she said. "Have you heard any buzz out there that could actually be useful?

"We can agree to disagree on the reality of Messie and the Priesthood. Beyond that, and the team formations going on, the most vocal have been Davey and Daisy, like Jack said. I still don't see them as killers, though." He stood and strolled to the store window looking out on the courtyard.

Morgan followed. The tables of the psychics had been rearranged, no doubt reflecting the newly formed alliances. The Rockets were set up next to each other and firmly planted in Janine's territory. Team Animal. "It makes sense they've aligned with the animal team since they had an issue with Edna. One that likely trickled over to Rocky. Guilt by association, you know?" She noticed Cal watching her intently. "What?"

"I have an idea. It's out there, but it might work."

"Please, after what I've heard about werewolves and sea creatures, how farfetched can your idea be?"

"We have a séance before the dinner tonight. We spread the word that Edna and Rocky will reveal who the killer is."

"Since we can't possibly guarantee that will happen, how is that supposed to help exactly?"

"I think the killer might likely show up to make sure no one actually identified them."

"This sounds a lot like your previous scheme at the writers retreat when you roped me into pretending I was an aspiring romance writer and convinced me to read the pages of that awful romance novel left by the killer to 'draw them out,'" she emphasized using air quotes. She crossed her arms and shook her head. "A dark room with a potential killer stalking the attending psychics? It's not just a bad idea, it's a terrible idea."

"Huh. I suppose there might be a wee similarity to last time. But I'm sure it'll work this time, though. You and JJ and the volunteer deputies can monitor the B&B and the perimeter of the room. Keep your eyes peeled for anything or anyone suspicious-looking."

"I suppose you had a 'premonition' about it?" Morgan scoffed. "No, Cal. Just no."

"We'll start at six. I'll tell the psychics to spread the word. Wear something black."

Damn Caleb Joseph. He completely ignored her and immediately went out to talk to the psychics. She should arrest him for interfering in police business. Just the idea of closing the cell door after stuffing him inside made her smile. Her stomach growled and she patted it. "You're right. We do need something chocolate and covered in buttercream."

"HANNAH, thank you for making the best cupcakes ever. You are a Bijoux treasure," Morgan said as Hannah filled a box of mixed sweets for her.

"You're kind to say so." Hannah smiled. "How are you doing, anyway? Lots of chatter around town and on the local news."

"You can ignore the local news. What have you heard from actual people and not Connie Graham? Because I'm pretty sure she's an alien sent to Earth with the explicit job of tormenting me."

Hannah laughed, then her blue eyes turned serious. "Depends on the visitor. Locals think they're safe since only psychics are dying. Tourists are mostly oblivious. The psychics, on the other hand, think there's going to be another murder." She shrugged. "At least that's what I've heard from the ones in here buzzing about." Hannah closed the pink box and tied it with a pretty yellow ribbon. "That won't happen, will it?"

"Not if I can prevent it." *I have to keep anything else bad from happening.*

"Morgan, we knew you'd be here," Zoe said as she and Rennie entered the bakery. "I wanted to show you my dress." She lifted the bag she was carrying and pointed with it to the table in the corner. "Join us for a moment?"

Morgan sat down at the table with the older women. "I wasn't sure you'd both still be talking to me after our earlier conversation."

"Nonsense," Rennie said patting her hand. "You're just doing your job. Besides, it's helped bring Jack and Starman together, given them a common enemy so to speak."

Morgan raised an eyebrow. "Really. How is it I keep getting made into the bad guy around here?"

"Well, you know what I mean." Rennie cleared her throat. "Zoe, why don't you show Morgan the dress."

Zoe stood and pulled a lavender charmeuse shift out of the bag. "Isn't it beautiful?" she whispered, running a hand over the silk fabric.

"It really is." Tears threatened and Morgan pushed them down. "I love it." She reached across the table and touched Zoe's hand. "You make my dad happy. Thank you for that."

Zoe started tearing up. Rennie poked at her. "Put the dress away or you'll stain it. Save the tears for tomorrow."

Zoe laughed and sat down, putting the dress back into the bag. "My sister, the hopeless romantic."

"I am forever hopeful, not hopeless, thank you very much." Rennie gave a firm nod. "Particularly so for you, dear sister. I love that you've found love again." She turned to Morgan and abruptly changed the subject. "I hear there's going to be a séance tonight."

"Yeah, but it's not real." Morgan opened the box and offered Zoe and Rennie each a cupcake. Both women declined. Morgan shrugged then plucked a double chocolate one and took a bite. She closed her eyes for a moment in delight.

"Of course it's not, it's designed to flush out the murderer, if I'm not mistaken," Rennie said. "Pretty good idea Cal has there. Of course, he only told us two about that angle." Rennie exchanged a smiled with Zoe. "If the spirits do show up — which is highly likely given the concentration of energies here — who are we to argue with them?"

Morgan swallowed another bite of cupcake and shook her head. "You believe Edna and Rocky might actually show up and reveal who the killer is?"

"Well, it could happen. It depends on how well a psychic interprets what the dead are trying to communicate," Zoe said. "A common misconception is when someone dies, they become all knowing. It's just not how it works, especially if they're still tied to the earth plane. That's why psychics are important. A good psychic can filter out the nonsense and see the light of truth."

"Look, I'm a cop. You get to the truth through investigation and gathering evidence. Factual evidence—not talking to dead people. Besides, seances aren't real," Morgan said, licking icing off her finger.

Rennie patted Morgan's shoulder, a twinkle in her eye. "If you say so, dear. If you say so."

CHAPTER 20

MORGAN LEFT HANNAH'S, her head spinning from a combination of sugar and random information about ghosts and seances. She grabbed her phone and called her deputy. "Hey, JJ. I'm going to need your help tonight."

"Sure. What's up?"

"Looks like there's going to be a séance at the Firefly, right before the closing banquet. Cal got a crazy idea he knows how to flush out the killer."

"I don't like it, doesn't seem smart to put all those people in potential danger." He was quiet for a breath. "But I'm guessing once he had the thought, you couldn't stop him."

"Short of locking him up and shutting down the event, which honestly I don't think would stop any of them. I decided to let it go and see if anything happens. Our leads are short, and you know how he is."

"That I do. Our professor has a stubborn streak, for sure. What time do you need me there?"

"It starts at six, so maybe thirty minutes ahead of that, so we can have a look around. And, I can't believe I'm going to say this, but what do you think about having the volunteer deputies on the bed and breakfast grounds?" Morgan asked.

"No concerns they might scare off our murderer? Assuming Cal's theory actually pans out."

"You've seen our volunteers, right?" Morgan laughed. "I don't think they could actually scare off anything." *Except potential dates*, she added silently.

"Okay, fine by me."

"Good because you're still officially in charge of them. I can't even with those three." She checked her watch. *Just enough time to get home and change, before we meet up at the Firefly.* "Gotta go. See you in a bit. Oh, and wear black. Apparently, that's a thing you do when attending a séance."

MORGAN HEARD Griselda howling as she walked up to her cottage. She unlocked the door and went in search of her houseguest. She found the cat in the back corner of the laundry room, staring at a blank corner, still howling like the devil was chasing her. Morgan scooped Gris up, gently flipped her on her back, and scratched the cat's stomach. "What's going on with you?" She scanned the small laundry room. "Did you see a mouse?" Gris angled her head and continued to stare at the wall. *Creepy cats and their creepy ways.* She lowered Gris to the floor. "Stop being spooky. Come on and I'll feed you. Give you something else to stare at."

With Griselda fed, Morgan caught her own self staring. Except it wasn't at a random corner, it was at her bedroom closet. She had a lot of black, but what was appropriate for a séance? *Wait, did I just think that?* She shook her head. All this psychic nonsense was obviously getting to her. She grabbed a pair of skinny black jeans, a black t-shirt, a thin black leather jacket and tossed them on, along with her black combat boots. She double checked the safety on her side arm and inserted it into the back holster she'd clipped on her pants. Morgan ran a hand through her dark hair, finger combing the choppy bob. Satisfied, she headed to the Firefly.

THE PARKING LOT was almost full, and Beau and Pete were attempting to direct cars away from the grass and onto a small gravel lot off to the street side. Morgan didn't see Mr. Dominic anywhere. *He must be inside.* She stopped and rolled down her window. "Has it been this busy since you guys got here? This is crazy."

"Sure has. Word got out ghosts might show up, maybe even a

werewolf, and the whole town suddenly turns up to see what all the fuss is about. We saved the spot with the cone over there for you."

"Oh, for heaven's sake. And thank you," she said as she angled the Ranger around a tight corner and slipped into the spot after Beau removed the orange cone.

The sounds inside the Firefly were deafening. There had to be about seventy-five people Morgan estimated, all milling in the small lobby. Off to the side was the banquet hall ante room where, according to the sign, the séance would be held. A small bar was set up next to the check in desk and a line had formed, wrapping around the bystanders.

"Here, I got this for you." Cal walked up and handed her a bottle of Lake M non-alcoholic Porter from one of the local microbreweries.

She took a drink and sighed. "Thank you. Not bad considering there's no alcohol."

"Well, you are on duty and I do know your rules about such things." He looked her up and down and grinned. "You are seriously bad ass in that outfit."

Morgan's stomach did a flip-flop, which she covered with exaggerated bravado. "I *am* bad ass, no matter the outfit. Never forget that." She turned her attention to the room, scanning the crowd. Starman and his son, Rob, were off in a corner, Rob looking around the room with a scowl on his face. She'd have to remember to check with JJ about his search on the guy. "So, tell me, what happens next?"

Cal checked his smart watch. "We gather the psychics into the ante room over there and get them in their seats. Once they're settled, we can invite the public in and get started. I thought I'd have the public hang around the perimeter of the room. That would put any visitors about fifteen feet away from the table. What do you think?"

"I think you're in charge of the psychics and should go manage them. Have you seen JJ? He was meeting me here."

"No, but that doesn't mean anything. This place is packed so unless he came looking for me, I don't know that I would've seen him. Okay gotta get things started."

Morgan nodded and Cal wended through the crowd and addressed the assembly.

Morgan texted her deputy. *What's your ETA?*

Be there in ten, he replied.

"Good evening, psychics and visitors," Cal shouted above the din. "Thank you for being here this evening for our First Annual *Walk into the Light Psychic Fair* Séance." He waited until the clapping died down, then continued, "Would all of the psychics please come into the ante room with me?" He walked toward the room and the readers followed.

"Caleb, what about us?" a non-psychic local asked. "We want to see the ghosts, too."

"We have a new pool going at the senior center about whether or not we'll see a werewolf tonight," Mr. Dominic called out. "I might be disqualified, though, since I'm here as a police officer." He hung his head and sighed.

"I'm not sure you being a volunteer deputy would have anything to do with it. Depends on the rules. But you should probably quit betting on stuff, Mr. D," Cal said to Dominic. To the others, he replied, "I'll call the public in as soon as we're set up and ready to go."

Murmurs of approval sounded around the lobby.

"Hey, sorry I'm late."

"What's up?" Morgan asked. JJ was almost always prompt.

"I had some info roll in on Davey Rocket and Daisy and wanted to vet it before talking to you."

Morgan motioned to the corridor off the lobby where no one was standing, and JJ followed. "What'd you find out?"

"They've been picked up more than once for criminal mischief relative to fortune telling."

"That's not surprising. It sounds like they've been doing this a long time." She shrugged. "There's bound to have been complaints."

"Sure, but the really interesting piece is Davey took a swing at a couple of officers a year ago. They called him a fraud and he didn't take kindly to it. He spent the night in jail. It was a small town in Ohio and they sent him packing, no charges pressed, just the report filed." JJ leaned in. "And, get this, apparently he told the cops when he was leaving he was going to make it his job to ferret out the real fakes. He was tired of being accused of something he wasn't."

Morgan thought about the implications. Davey was angry with

Edna and maybe it went deeper than a camp site argument. "What are you thinking? He's turned vigilante and wants to remove the frauds permanently to prove he's the real thing?' She took a sip of her drink. "It's a bit of a stretch, but maybe... We'll have to do some digging, see if we can place him in Traverse City and Detroit at the time of the other murders."

"I stopped at the station before I came here and started some searches running, looking for psychic events around the same time the others were killed."

Morgan smiled. "Good work. Did you pick up anything on Starman's son?"

JJ shook his head. "Nothing incriminating, beyond his vocal proclamations that psychics aren't real."

"Okay." Morgan noticed the crowd was moving. "Let's go. Looks like they're going to start the séance."

The ante room was set up with several tables in the middle, arranged to make a large square with a space in the center, with enough seats for all the psychics. The lights were dimmed, the tables were covered with red cloths, and a profusion of candles cast light all around. There was a white tablecloth on the floor in the center of the tables.

"What do you think that's for?" JJ asked.

Morgan shrugged. "In case the ghost is naked...?"

JJ gave a low laugh. "Well, we've heard stranger things this week."

Morgan noticed not all the psychics were participating. Team Animal was conspicuously missing and gathered off to the side. "Then there's that," she said, motioning to the small group. Janine, Sven, Daisy, Davey, and a couple of others whose names she didn't know. "Keep an eye on them, please."

"I'm on it," JJ said and began working his way through the crowd to the other side of the room.

"Everyone who is not participating in the séance, please gather at the perimeter of the room. We want to make sure no one feels crowded."

"Especially the spirits," Rennie said from her seat. "And please know they won't like it if people try to touch them or talk to them

135

outside of the ones in this circle." She motioned around the table. "So please keep your distance and do not interfere."

James the desk clerk stood at the double doorway. "Zoe Buffett? Is there a Zoe Buffett here?"

Zoe got up from her seat opposite Rennie. "I'm Zoe. How can I help you?"

"Message for you, ma'am." His eyes darted around the room as he handed her a folded piece of paper, then he hurried back out the door. Morgan envied him.

Zoe looked at the paper and then met her sister's eyes. "Rennie, I'll be back in a few. Go ahead and start. I'll rejoin as soon as I can."

Rennie tilted her head. "You're sure about this?" she asked.

Zoe nodded. "I'm sure."

"Everything okay?" Morgan asked.

Zoe looked up at Morgan. "Of course, why wouldn't it be?" She tucked the paper in her dress pocket and patted Morgan's arm. "

"Let us begin, then," Rennie said. "All of you participating, join hands above the table. Right hand on top, left hand on bottom."

"I wonder what that's about?" Morgan murmured to herself.

"It's how energy flows," a male voice whispered in her ear.

Morgan jumped, hand to her heart. "I swear to god, Cal, if you come up on me like that one more time, I *will* shoot you."

"Well, we all know how I like to live dangerously." He wiggled his eyebrows. "About the hands—the right hand sends energy and the left hand receives. It creates a circuit within the circle."

"Could we have quiet, please?" Rennie asked. "All of you around the room, please refrain from comments or questions until the séance is completed. Now, we will begin." She looked around the table. "Brothers and Sisters, repeat after me: Our beloved Edna and Rocky, we bring you gifts from life into death. Commune with us, dearest Edna and Rocky, and move amongst us." Rennie spoke the incantation three times. "Now, we wait," she whispered.

The room was completely quiet, except for breathing and a few quiet whispers. Morgan checked her watch and noted ten minutes had passed when a huge wind blew through the room and extinguished at least half of the candles. "What the hell?"

"Looks like the spirits have landed," Cal whispered. "Should be interesting. I've never actually witnessed a séance before."

Someone screamed from the other side of the room.

Morgan rushed over to JJ who was crouched down near what appeared to be a prone figure.

"Where are you, Davey Rocket? I know you're the murderer!" Jack yelled. He stood and stepped into the crowd.

"How dare you?!?" Davey yelled back as he stepped forward from the back of Team Animal. He squinted at Jack. "Just like you, trying to dodge the cops by pointing the finger at someone else."

Jack drew himself up as Morgan stepped between the men, separating them. "Not now!" She pushed them out of the way and went back to JJ.

"Someone get the lights," Rennie shouted.

The lights came on and Morgan sighed as she squatted down, checked the old man's wrist for a pulse. "Mr. Dominic, are you okay?"

He was clutching his chest and breathing rapidly.

Cal made his way to their side, his phone in his hand. "I'm on with 911."

Mr. Dominic held out a hand. "No, no, not necessary."

Morgan helped him sit up. "What happened?" she asked, noticing the color was slowly returning to his face. She shook her head at Cal who ended the 911 call and slipped the phone back in his pocket.

"I guess I got scared when that wind blew through. Never felt such a breeze as cold as that. Death's icy fingers is what it was, coming for me." Mr. Dominic held his hands out and wiggled his bony fingers. "Just like that. Coming for me..."

Morgan felt another blast of wind and looked up. They were directly under a ceiling air conditioning vent. "It was the A/C. Someone must've cranked up the fan on the unit. Nothing more. Are you sure you don't want us to call for help?"

"I'm fine." He got to his feet and shook his fist at the air vent. "You're not gonna get me today, icy fingers. Not today."

"Did anyone see Zoe return?" Rennie asked from her seat at the table.

Everyone looked around the room, shaking their heads. "Haven't seen her since she left right after that desk clerk," Janine said.

"Do you think he's the werewolf?" Sven asked. "My vibes are off right now. Could be him as much as anyone, I suppose," Janine said. "It's like this room is energetically locked down, though. I got nothing." Rennie stared at Morgan and their eyes met. Morgan nodded. "Come on, JJ. Let's have a look around." Cal was right behind them.

CHAPTER 21

"JAMES, do you know where Zoe went?" Morgan asked the front desk clerk. He looked blankly at her. "The woman you brought the note to."

"Oh, oh yeah. She went down that way." He pointed to the hallway opposite the ante room where the séance had been held.

"Was she with anyone?" JJ asked.

"No, sir. By herself."

"Who gave you the note?" Cal asked.

"No idea, actually. I went over to clear glasses from the side table over there." James pointed across to the lounge. "When I came back to the counter, it was here with her name on it." He shrugged and looked at Cal. "Yours is the only event going on, so I figured she must be in there."

"Thank you," Morgan said and made her way down the hallway with JJ and Cal in tow.

"This is weird," JJ said. "I don't have a good feeling about this."

Morgan shook her head and rolled her eyes. "Are you becoming psychic too, JJ?"

"Well, why did she leave suddenly like that when she knows there's a killer on the loose?"

Morgan was worried. She should have gone after Zoe. But maybe the note had been from Able. Still, Morgan should have insisted on reading the note. She'd been so preoccupied with the séance and possibly exposing the killer she didn't consider they might have used the séance to lure out their next victim. "I wish people would take the threat around here seriously," She muttered. "Honestly, it's exhausting.

"I hear that," Cal said from behind. "Humans make me tired."

"*You* make me tired," Morgan threw back, then she held up her hand and they stopped. They were nearing the end of the corridor. "I hear voices," she said.

Cal lifted an eyebrow and his lips twitched.

"Not those kinds of voices." She huffed and started walking again. "I am so going to lock you up when we're done with this case. Before you ask—Yes, for annoying the police captain. That's a thing now."

JJ snickered as they stopped in front of a closed door.

"That's definitely Zoe's voice," Morgan said. She couldn't make out the other voice, it was too muffled. She raised her hand to knock when the door creaked open.

Morgan gasped at what she saw.

"My God," Cal uttered.

"Captain," JJ whispered.

CHAPTER 22

ZOE STOOD IN THE DOORWAY, her eyes wide, a rope looped tight around her neck. A man's hands held tight to the rope from behind. Morgan couldn't make out his face. The room was dark and he was crouching behind Zoe.

"Zoe," Morgan said as calmly as she could. She had to do whatever it took to keep the situation from escalating. While whoever was back there had no way to escape, it didn't mean he couldn't do any damage before they took him down. It didn't take much to snap a neck if you're an experienced killer. "What's going on with your friend there?"

"He asked for a reading." Zoe's eyes darted side to side as if she were trying to see her captor. "I knew I was the one he's been searching for, so I obliged."

Searching for? That made no sense. "I'm not sure what you're talking about."

"He's distressed and hasn't been able to find anyone who could help him."

"And did you? Help him with a reading?" Morgan asked.

"Not yet. We heard all of you out in the hallway. JJ and Cal, you're not very stealthy, you know, despite what you may tell yourselves. This gentleman thought it would be a good idea to use me for leverage."

"She's probably a fraud, anyway," the man muttered from behind Zoe.

There was that word again, *fraud*. Morgan angled her head but he'd turned his face away. "Is that you, Rob? You know lawyers never do well in prison."

"You really are horrible with names. It's not *Rob*."

141

"Well, how about you let her go and we can talk? You can enlighten me."

"How stupid do you think I am? This rope stays in place. All of you, stay out there in the hallway while I get my reading. After I hear what she has to say, I'll consider letting her go." He pulled the rope a little tighter and Zoe coughed. "Assuming she's the real thing, that is. In my experience, it's unlikely, but I'll give her the benefit of the doubt. I always do."

As he spoke, Zoe's eyes went blank. And, as much as Morgan hated knowing the reason for it, she knew a message was coming through.

"Trent Tracy Lang!" Zoe's voice boomed.

The man straightened to his full height, his eyes wide, but hands still tight on the rope. The hallway light hit his face. "I didn't tell you my name."

Wait. The Garanimal guy? He was still dressed in matching clothes, denim from head to toe, with a navy-blue *Traverse City Save the Dachshunds* tee under his shirt. Everything he wore was some shade of blue, even the dog printed on his tee. *Seriously? This is the blue animal?* Zoe had said only Morgan would understand the messages given. She shook her head to clear it. Zoe was throwing the guy off. Maybe she could use it to her advantage. "Trent? I thought your name was Elvis. And what's up with the dachshund rescue?"

"Why would you think that? Honestly, I've told you my name at least twice now." He sneered at her. He was standing beside Zoe now, his hands still holding tight to the rope. "What sort of police officer can't remember names?" He shrugged. "The shirt is a family thing, if you must know."

"Trent. We have to talk about what you did." Zoe's voice was deep and commanding. "Let me look at you." He allowed her to turn as he held the rope in place. Her eyes remained blank.

"Who are you?" he asked.

Zoe snorted, shaking her head. "You were never the smartest child, were you?"

"Dad...?"

Zoe glanced at Morgan, Cal, and JJ, eyes still blank, but her expression animated. "It's the reason I changed my will, you understand. He couldn't be trusted with the family money." Zoe looked back at Trent. "I *told* you that was the reason when you came to see me that day."

"What I know is you listened to a psychic who told you to cut me out. Believed a *fraud* over your own son. Then you chose these freaking dachshunds over me." He jabbed at his chest. "Honestly, how could you do that? Don't you see how hurtful you've been?"

"You could never see the helplessness in others, the need, above your own selfishness. You are not helpless and it was time you learned to stand on your own two feet. Really, I should've cut you off much sooner." Zoe looked him up and down, frowning. "Maybe you would have grown a backbone."

"You're just as horrible dead as you were alive," Trent spat.

"And we both know how I died, don't we?"

"How did you die?" Morgan asked, then mentally checked herself for encouraging the whole charade. Though, she had to admit, what Zoe was saying seemed to be striking a chord with Trent.

"Trent knows." Zoe tilted her head. "He will not speak of it, though. He's too afraid."

Trent's eyes filled with tears. "I carry the guilt of it with me every day." He looked at Morgan, JJ, and Cal. "I want you to know that."

"What guilt, buddy?" JJ asked. "Maybe we can help you with it."

"Yeah, there's no helping me at this point." Trent gave a desperate laugh and shook his head. "Dad called me over that day to say he'd written me out of the will and was donating everything to his dachshund rescue project." He uncoiled the rope and slumped on the edge of the bed.

Morgan wrapped her arm around Zoe who was breathing heavily and gently pulled her away from Trent.

JJ made a move toward Trent, but Morgan touched his arm to stop him. "Let him talk."

"We fought about it. Dad dangled the old will in front of me, was going to throw it in the fireplace. I shoved him, hard, and made a grab for it. Knocked him over. His head slammed against the hearth."

"Sounds like an accident," JJ said.

"It was. Sort of," Trent said. He shrugged. "Until it wasn't."

"He left me there, bleeding out while he burned the new will.

Intentionally let me die. Intentionally let his own father die...." Zoe's voice drifted off and she began to cough as her hands rubbed her neck.

Trent looked at her, surprised. "Wait. You saw that? I thought you were unconscious."

"I was hovering above my body, witnessed all of it." Tears ran down Zoe's cheeks. "And I want you to know, I've let go of my anger. I forgive you, my boy." With this last statement, Zoe tilted, unsteady, and Cal caught her before she crumpled to the floor. She whispered to Cal and he looked at Morgan, who nodded, having heard what Zoe wanted to do. JJ moved to block the door and Cal held Zoe's arm as she moved closer to Trent. She sat beside him on the bed and reached out, laying a hand on Trent's cheek. "He loved you very much, he just wasn't good at showing it."

"*You* are *not* a fraud," Trent whispered, tears streaming down his cheeks. "You are the real thing. No strikes against you. You get to live." Tears ran down his cheeks and he tossed the rope on the floor. "Thank you for seeing my pain." He looked up. "And my guilt."

Morgan and JJ escorted Trent, in handcuffs, down the hall and through the lobby of the Firefly, Cal helping Zoe along behind them. Team Edna and Team Rocky were lined up on either side with Team Animal closest to the door.

"He doesn't look like an animal," Janine sniffed. "But he is blue."

"It's not the full moon yet," Sven offered. "Maybe he gets meaner and hairier the closer we get to it."

Rennie retrieved Zoe from Cal and looked her sister over. She hugged her tight. "You're all right."

Zoe smiled. "That I am." She looked over at Trent, her eyes filled with tears. "But he's most definitely not. I'm not sure he ever was or ever will be."

CHAPTER 23

MORGAN AND JJ drove Trent to the police station while Cal stayed behind to get the psychics settled in for their closing night banquet. Once they had Trent secured, JJ started the arrest paperwork. He also placed calls to Traverse City and Detroit to let them know the suspect was detained. "Hey, Cap'n. Detroit claimed first jurisdiction and is sending someone in the morning to pick Trent up."

"Thanks, JJ." Morgan lingered by the cell, watching. "Why Zoe?" she asked her prisoner.

Trent ignored her from where he sat on the tiny cot and dropped his head in his hands.

"I asked you a question. Why Zoe? All these psychics in one place, why did you choose her this time?" Morgan asked.

"I've been watching her the entire event. I asked around. People talked about how good she is. But people always talk without actually knowing things, don't they? They thought Edna and Rocky were good, but they were hacks. So I had to see for myself."

"You were going to kill her."

"Maybe. I don't know." He shook his head. "You wouldn't understand."

She crossed her arms and leaned against the bars. "Try me."

He let out a long breath. "I didn't set out to kill my father that day, but it happened all the same. Believe it or not, I was consumed with guilt, but terrified to admit what I'd done. Dad frequented psychics, believed wholeheartedly in their ability to tell the future. I thought maybe one of them could see what I was going through."

The pieces started falling together. "You wanted to be outed for your crime?"

Trent nodded. "Yeah, basically."

145

"Okay, but why kill those psychics? And why call them frauds? What happened to make you angry enough to go after them?"

He stood and started pacing the small cell, rubbing his face, running his hands through his hair. "Because they *were* frauds! Not one of them could see beyond the standard crap— Oh, look, you're going to find love, have amazing friends, and be happy forever," he finished in a sing-song voice. Trent plopped back down on the cot. "Please. Do I honestly look like that kind of person?"

Morgan had to agree with him. Sadly, he did not look like he'd ever known happiness or love. "Just because they're not any good, it doesn't mean you should have killed them."

"Of course I did. You just don't get it."

"Educate me."

"They had no business claiming the mantle of psychic." His eyes met Morgan's. "What sort of person would I be if I left them to lie to others like they lied to me?"

Ah, here's the crazy I knew was there if I dug around enough. "We'll get you some dinner in a bit. But don't get too comfortable. You're leaving in the morning."

THE NEXT DAY, Morgan arrived at the station early to hand off Trent to the officer from Detroit. She checked her watch. A black SUV pulled up and parked along the curb. Nine a.m. Right on time.

"Hey, officer."

Morgan knew that voice. "Liz! What are you doing here?" She rushed to her friend and hugged her.

"I convinced the detective in charge of this case to let me make the trip." Liz held Morgan at arm's length and smiled. "Small town life seems to agree with you. Well, besides the murders and all."

"Don't get me started. It's been good and horrifying here all at the same time. But four deaths in three months is a bit much." She sighed. "I mean, it's great to be back home. Dad and I are doing really good." Morgan smacked her forehead. "Oh my god. He's getting married this afternoon. You have to stay for the wedding."

"I actually planned on hanging around overnight so we could catch up. I was hoping that'd be okay and it sounds like it is." Liz smiled. "Need a date?"

Morgan laughed. "You know I always do." She linked her arm with her friend's. "Come on inside. Let's get the transfer paperwork out of the way. Then we'll go to my place and get ready for the ceremony."

CHAPTER 21

IT WAS late afternoon and Morgan stood beside her dad, their arms draped over each other's shoulder, both dressed in black tuxes with light gray shirts and purple ties. "Looks like a great turnout," she said. "Thanks for making me your best man."

"I'm grateful you're here, back in my life." Able wiped at his eyes and squeezed his daughter to him. "Besides, who else would I pick?" He laughed and shook his head. "If you had told me just a few years ago I'd be remarrying *and* it would be to a psychic witch, I'd have called BS on you right then and there."

Morgan laughed, too, and patted his back. The friends and family gathered were, indeed, a colorful group. Zoe's friends from the *Walk into the Light* gathering, her sister Rennie from neighboring Lac Voo — who was currently shooing a stray sea gull away from the seats before taking her place on the bride's side of the makeshift altar — the Bijoux locals, Cal sitting with Liz and Frankie and looking fancy in a dark gray suit with a purple handkerchief artfully poking from his breast pocket. Standing at the middle of the dais, where vows would be spoken, was Jack Steve dressed in a navy pinstripe suit and looking every bit the officiant.

Guitar strumming began and the first notes of the theme song from the old movie, *Love Story* floated around them. A barefoot Zoe, silver hair piled high on her head, dressed in her lavender charmeuse shift, and holding a bouquet of native wildflowers, appeared from behind a bamboo screen at the back of the aisle. She smiled at Morgan, winked at Able, then slowly walked toward her soon to be husband.

Able sniffed and Morgan squeezed his arm. "Are you ready?" she asked.

He smiled. "That I am. Let's do this."

THIRTY MINUTES LATER, after they'd spoken the vows they'd written, Jack Steve pronounced them husband and wife. The crowd clapped and cheered as the couple walked back down the aisle to James Taylor's, '*You've got a Friend.*'

"Come one everyone," Able called out. "Join us in celebrating with Hannah's heavenly red velvet cupcakes and champagne."

"No coffee cake?" Morgan asked, laughing, as she hugged her dad. She turned to Zoe and hugged her, too. "Welcome to the family."

"Congratulations, you two," Rennie said as she joined them. She had another woman with her Morgan didn't know, but she could've been a younger version of Rennie and Zoe. "Able, I don't think you've met our niece. This is Kate O'Connell. She owns A Brush with Coffee gallery and cafe in Lac Voo." Rennie beamed at her. "Helluva an artist, too."

"I can attest to that," Cal said. He carried a tray of champagne flutes and passed them around. "She did the painting of the Raven's Nest hanging up in the bookstore. Good to see you again, Kate," he said as he hugged her with one arm.

"That's why your name is familiar," Morgan said. She held out her hand and smiled. "I'm Morgan. Able's daughter. It's nice to meet you."

"You as well," Kate said shaking hands. Then she turned to Zoe. "Aunt Zoe! You look so beautiful." Kate beamed at her aunt and hugged her tight. She turned to Able, who held his arms out to her. "As do you, Uncle Able."

Able laughed. "Who knew I could be beautiful?"

"Well, I did, that's for sure." Arnie Hart, Able's twin brother, walked up and clapped Able on the back. He winked at Morgan and gave her a hug. "It runs in the family."

Cal offered a flute to Arnie and raised his. "A toast to the happy couple. May your days be filled with love and friendship, may you never find yourself wanting, may you always have whatever you need, especially each other."

Zoe sniffled. "What a lovely toast. Thank you, Caleb." Her eyes shimmered with tears and Able wrapped his arm around her waist and handed her his handkerchief.

THE RECEPTION WENT on into an evening filled with friends, family, and music. It was a beautiful night on the beach, the lake rushing in and out, a fat waxing moon lighting the sky. Morgan, Cal, Frankie, and Liz sat around a table near the edge of the dance area. Morgan had kicked off her heels and was digging her toes into the sand.

"You'll ruin that pedicure," Frankie said. She looked at Liz. "Not that she ever really cared about her toes. This one hates shoes and would go barefoot year-round if she could."

Liz laughed. "You should've seen her when the stripper showed up for her going away party if you want to talk about things she really doesn't like."

"Who doesn't like a good stripper?" Frankie asked, giggling.

"Exactly my thought when I hired him," Liz said, raising her wine glass in a toast toward Morgan.

Morgan just smiled as she watched her two best friends. She had a feeling when she introduced them they might just click with each other. *Well, that is if I believed in psychic premonitions.* But the idea of it made her happy. It was, after all, a night for love.

"Frankie Whitaker. We need to talk," Mayor Ed said as he approached the table.

"Yeah, no. It's not a good time." Frankie made a sweeping gesture. "We're at a wedding reception, if you hadn't noticed."

"Of course, I noticed. I'm not a fool. You've been avoiding my phone calls and whenever I stop by you always seem to be out running errands. I just want you to know I will be proposing legislation at our next town council meeting requiring all shopkeepers to comply with the new Bijoux Beautification Ordinance. I hope to see you there, Ms. Whitaker. You too, Caleb." He turned to Morgan. "Good to see you. Nice work on the case," he added then sauntered off.

"What's that about?" Liz asked.

"We have two divisions in Bijoux," Morgan said. "Those who are updating and renovating buildings on Main Street and what some call the 'Hold Outs.' The businesses who want to preserve our rundown lakeside charm." She looked at Frankie. "No offense. You know I love your rundown place."

"None taken." She sighed. "Guess I'll be going to battle again."

Morgan realized Cal had been unusually quiet throughout the encounter. "What are you thinking?" she asked. "You're considered a Hold Out too, so this affects you and the Raven's Nest."

"I'm thinking maybe I should run for mayor," Cal said.

"That would be the best thing ever!" Frankie exclaimed and clapped her hands together. She turned to Liz. "Cal here used to teach at U of M. He's level-headed *and* isn't a jerk. He'd have to do a better job than Ed Peltier has done lately."

"Um, thanks…?"

"Well, it's something to consider," Morgan said. "Though, you know, it could randomly put us on the opposite sides of things. And you wouldn't be able to tag along if something happens."

"Not true." He lifted an eyebrow. "As mayor, I would set the rules, so I could make it mandatory you have to let me ride shotgun."

Liz turned to Frankie and whispered loud enough that Morgan heard. "What's going on with these two?"

"Something they're both too stubborn to admit," she answered.

"Hey, Morgan. Dance with me."

Morgan looked up. Beau Cornet strode toward them, a beer in one hand and a plate of cake in the other.

"Sorry, Beau, she's taken for this dance," Cal said as he stood and held out his hand.

"Huh." Beau eyed Liz. Liz just shook her head. He shrugged. "Okay then," he said and walked away.

Cal continued to hold out his hand. "Morgan?"

"We don't have to actually dance. He's gone now," she said, even as she stood, took his hand in hers, and allowed herself to be led to the dance floor. *Moondance* by Van Morrison started playing. "I've always loved this song," Morgan said.

Cal slipped an arm around her waist and pulled her close. "Me too." He chuckled. "You know you owe me, once again, for rescuing you from an unwanted suitor."

Morgan smiled. "How about I just don't lock you up for all the times I should have?"

"Fair enough." Cal grinned at her. "Though locking me up would certainly add to the roguish resume I'm building to support my new mystery writing career."

"Excuse me?" Morgan almost choked, she laughed so hard. "Roguish resume? Who talks like that?"

Cal spun her at arm's length, then pulled her in tight. She felt his eyes on her soul, hated it — and didn't — all at the same time. *Damn him.*

"The man who's holding you, that's who."

A NOTE FROM TERI BARNETT

I hope you enjoyed *Mystics are Murder*, Book 2 in the Bijoux Mystery Series!

If you'd like to leave a review, which I would greatly appreciate, please visit amazon.com.

I love to hear from readers! You can contact me through my website at www.teribarnett.com. While you're there, please go ahead and subscribe to my newsletter so you can stay up to date on new releases, special offers, and giveaways.

Keep reading for a Sneak Peek of *Cupcakes are Murder*, Bijoux Mystery Series: Book 3!

Sneak Peek
Cupcakes are Murder
Bijoux Mystery Series: Book 3

"Officer down."

The call every cop dreads hearing.

Morgan Hart rushed to the address given over the car radio, her heart in her throat. She'd been out on a lunch run for her and her partner, Liz Shore. A wave of panic washed over Morgan as she turned onto the street. She had no explanation for it, but it took her breath away. Pulling up to the location, she saw her husband Ian's truck parked at the curb.

Maybe Ian was in the area? Maybe he heard the same call I did. Maybe he got here just before me....

But the anxiety, now laced with fear, grew and intensified when she locked eyes with Liz. Her partner of five years and dear friend rushed to stop her from going into the alley. James Wheat, Ian's partner, blocked Morgan after she pushed past Liz.

"You don't want to see this," James whispered harshly.

Morgan shoved him aside and ran down the alley. She stopped and froze, staring down at the sheet-draped body, a pool of blood soaked the ground around it.

Morgan looked up at Rosanna Jensen, the medical examiner. Her eyes pleaded with the older woman. *Please!* The word was lodged in her throat.

Rosanna nodded and pulled the sheet back.

Single gunshot wound to the chest.

He would've died instantly, felt nothing.

Morgan crumpled to the ground, feeling everything.

"Ian!" she screamed.

I'm here. The strong arms enveloped her, held her tight.

"Don't leave me," Morgan murmured, wrapping her arms around him.

I'm sorry....

"No. Please."

I have to go. You can't live in the past, Fay. You have to unlock it and let it go. I love you...

"Don't leave—" Morgan's eyes flew open, her arms tightly gripping her pillow, her legs tangled in the sheets. Ian was the only one who ever called her by her middle name, *Fay*. She sat upright, disoriented. Looked around her bedroom, her eye caught the clock. 3 a.m. She shoved her choppy brunette hair out of her eyes.

So real. So close.

Griselda, her black cat, was sitting at the foot of the bed, watching her.

"C'mere Gris," Morgan patted her leg and the large feline climbed into her lap. Morgan had adopted the Maine Coon after the cat's fortune-telling owner was murdered a couple of months ago. Gris placed a paw on her hand and began purring. Morgan took a steadying breath, cradled Gris close, and lay back down. A single tear ran down her cheek.

"How am I supposed to let him go when his murderer is still out there?" Morgan whispered into the cat's soft fur.

Gris mewed.

Morgan sighed and settled back under the covers of her bed in the cozy beachside cottage she inherited from her late mom, Billie. Gris curled up tighter beside her.

I came back to Bijoux to get away from a stressful and complicated life and now it feels like I've gone and stepped into another one.

Her return to her hometown was supposed to be easy, a fresh start, a small town with a slower pace. And a chance for Morgan to untangle her life from her past as a homicide detective in Detroit. And more importantly, a way to try to let go of the pain of Ian's murder and her mom, Billie's, death from colon cancer a few years ago.

At Able's encouragement, Morgan moved back to Bijoux to take on the job of police captain, a job her dad had held for thirty-plus years. "Nothing ever happens in Bijoux," he told her. "You know that kiddo." Morgan had had a strained relationship with her dad over the years, after her parents divorced when Morgan was just fourteen. Her move back home was supposed to be a new beginning for the two of them as well.

She was pleasantly surprised to find Able had moved on after his split with Billie and he'd found love again and married Zoe Buffet. Together, the two of them took over Hal's Hardware Store, turning it into one of the main gathering places in Bijoux.

Then, on her first day on the job, a murder. Three more followed over the summer. The first ones Bijoux had seen in almost a hundred years and they were happening on her watch.

Unacceptable.

Dreams. Nightmares. They were all the same, whether she slept or didn't sleep. She was increasingly tired. Exhausted. Most nights spent tossing and turning, intent on solving the cases in front of her. Intent on solving Ian's murder from five years ago. Her husband had been working undercover. The investigative officers declared it a drug deal gone bad.

Morgan had other ideas.

"I will not let go, Ian," she whispered as her eyelids grew heavy once more. "Not until I find your killer."

"Whoa, Cap'n," JJ said as Morgan walked into the station. It was Thursday morning and Jeremy Jones, aka JJ, the solid, five-foot-ten, red-headed deputy was leaning against the worn oak front counter, talking to his girlfriend, Hannah Bellamy of Hannah's Heavenly Confections. Hannah was also a red head but almost a foot shorter and a lot curvier.

"What?" Morgan's eyes narrowed, daring him to speak.

JJ held up his hands. "Nothing. You just look like you've been wrestling Griselda." He grimaced. "And Gris won."

Morgan took a sip from the to-go cup of rich, black coffee she'd picked up at Dave's Deli on the way to work. Jerome, the ever opinionated waiter, had commented about her appearance, too, only he went into great detail about the puffiness around her eyes and possible remedies.

"What you look like is you could use one of these." Hannah opened the magenta and green polka-dotted box sitting on the counter and lifted out a cupcake. "Triple Mochaccino." She smiled as she handed the work of culinary art to Morgan. "Dark chocolate cake, whipped milk chocolate frosting, coffee crème center. And vanilla sprinkles."

"Oh, my goodness. I've already had breakfast, but I can definitely make room for one of these." Morgan closed her eyes and all but purred as she inhaled the aroma of rich chocolate and coffee in her hand. She peeled back a bit of the delicate turquoise paper and took a bite of cake and frosting. Just the perfect amount of each. "Hannah, would you like to be my new deputy?" Morgan looked over at JJ. "There's going to be an opening for that position very soon." She took another small bite. "You will, of course, have to bring these in every day."

Hannah laughed. "Thanks, but I have my hands full with the bakery."

"Seriously, Cap'n," JJ said. "Are you all right? Because you don't look all right."

Morgan paused mid-bite and stared at him over the top of the cupcake. "Do you have a death wish today?"

"Who has a death wish?" Caleb Joseph asked as he strolled into the station. The six-foot two, dark-haired owner of The Raven's Nest Bookstore, former U of M English lit professor, and best-selling, gothic romance writer (under a *nom de plume*), flashed a grin. "And should I be worried?"

"It's not always about you, Cal." Morgan glanced over at him, noticed he was wearing faded jeans that molded to his lean legs and a red-plaid flannel shirt today, the sleeves rolled to his elbows. *Interesting*. Cal never dressed down.

Cal glanced back, then stopped and looked her up and down. "Damn, Morgan. I know it's been challenging with those murder cases since you got here, but you probably should try to look, well…."

She scowled at him. "Look like what, exactly?"

"Less like the cat won?" he offered.

"That's exactly what I said!" JJ grinned.

"What is wrong with you people?" Morgan looked down at herself. Okay, maybe her blue and khaki uniform wasn't as freshly pressed as usual, and maybe she'd neglected to use the lint brush this morning after giving Gris a cuddle before she left, and maybe her sleep was riddled with nightmares lately. But that didn't mean anything. She sighed, tucked a wayward strand of hair behind an ear and picked a fluff of cat fur off her pant leg. "I'm fine. Why do you guys insist on getting into my business? I promise, I'll tell you if I need help."

"No, you won't," Cal countered. "That's not who you are, Captain Morgan."

Morgan shrugged and took another bite of the cupcake. *There. Cupcakes make everything better.*

"You're eating it wrong," Cal said.

Morgan's brows lifted. "I beg your pardon?"

"Everyone knows you eat a cupcake from the bottom up. Save the frosting and sprinkles for last." Cal looked at Hannah. "Am I mistaken?"

Hannah shook her head. "I am not getting in the middle of this argument. Been there, done that."

"JJ?"

"Actually, you'd be wrong there, Cal." JJ picked up a cupcake with vanilla Swiss meringue frosting and silver sprinkles. It looked like a mini-wedding cake. "Being the stuffy professor you are, I can see why you'd think starting with the cake is better, since that's boring. The truth is, you dive headfirst into the icing, then top it off with the cake and a glass of ice cold milk." He took a giant bite, leaving frosting on both sides of his mouth. Hannah giggled and handed him a napkin.

"You're both ridiculous," Morgan interjected. "You eat them simul-taneously. That way you get the best of both worlds, at the same time." She shook her head. "I don't know what's wrong with you two. And I mean that on a lot of levels."

"Well, you'll soon have the opportunity to ask the cupcake queen herself the best way to eat one of these," Cal said, holding up his caramel drizzled milk chocolate cupcake with whipped cherry buttercream frosting.

"Hannah has already refused to participate in this discussion," Morgan said around another bite, washing it down with a sip of coffee.

Hannah laughed. "While I appreciate you think I'm the queen, there's only one true cupcake queen and that'd be Sassy McComas. Her fans call her Queen Sass. And she's the founder of Queenie's Loquacious Cakes. She's from the UK but made her baking name here in the States on the Baking Network." Hannah clapped her hands together. "She's my idol. I still can't believe she's bringing her Baker's Dozen Hometown Cupcake Bake-off right here to Bijoux!"

"That's this week already?" Morgan asked. It wasn't like her to forget something as important as an event that could bring hundreds of outsiders to Bijoux. Potential trouble for her small town, especially since Cal was organizing it and murder seemed to happen at every event he touched. First it was the romance writers' conference, then the psychic fair. And with the highly anticipated contest coming up, Morgan was worried about a killer triple hat trick.

I need to get myself together. She glanced at Cal, saw the worry in his eyes, and decided to ignore it.

"You do remember Hannah and I entered Bijoux in the Baker's Dozen Bake-off for a chance to host the competition, right?" Cal asked. "And we won."

"Of course, I do," Morgan replied. "Tell me, does that have anything to do with why you're dressed like a lumberjack?"

"Ah, deflecting. This I can deal with. Yes, it's why I'm *casually* dressed. The Raven's Nest is, of course, Bijoux's main sponsor of the event. Plus, I'm helping to get things set up at the community center. We've enlisted some of the art students from the high school, too. They're painting a mural of giant confections on one side of the building. Dancing cakes and things." He paused. "No porn star mustaches, though. I was pretty clear that was a no-go."

Morgan snorted. Her first day back in Bijoux, besides dealing with the murder of a famous romance writer, found her and JJ investigating a graffiti 'artist' who was going around painting giant Tom Selleck-esque mustaches on everything.

"And you thought you'd dress like them?" JJ interjected. "Dude, you look like one of the Village People."

Cal carefully placed his cupcake on the counter, stepped to the center of the space, did a spin and then spelled out the Y M C A letters with his arms. He gave a slight bow as Hannah clapped and hooted, then walked back over and continued eating his cupcake. From the bottom up.

JJ whistled. "I did not see that coming."

"No one did, JJ." Morgan just stared at Cal. "No one did."

I hope you enjoyed this sneak peek of
Cupcakes are Murder
Bijoux Mystery Series: Book 3

Visit Amazon.com to purchase your copy!

ABOUT THE AUTHOR

Teri Barnett is the author of the Bijoux Mystery Series and the upcoming Lac Voo Mystery Series as well as numerous non-fiction books about Reiki. In a past life, she also wrote historical time-travel/paranormal romance (check out her Oracle Dreams Trilogy).

In addition to writing, Teri is an award-winning artist and nationally recognized commercial interior designer who brings a lifetime of learning and exploration to her writing and workshops. Born and raised in Michigan, Teri currently resides in Indiana where she writes books, does cool art, crochets too many shawls and afghans, and hangs out with Black Cat Lou, her bossy black cat. Though not a Maine Coon, BCL *is* the inspiration for Morgan's rescue cat, Griselda, who makes her debut in Book 2, Mystics are Murder.

When Teri isn't busy working on her next book or redesigning the world, you can find her doing the artist thing in her studio (painting or designing book covers), tromping through the forest, hanging with her kids and grandbabies, or riding through the corn tunnels of Indiana on her motorcycle.

You can visit Teri online at www.teribarnett.com to learn more about her books, contact her, and/or subscribe to her newsletter. Want to follow Lou's antics? You can find her on Insta @TheBlackCatLou.

ALSO BY TERI BARNETT

BIJOUX MYSTERY SERIES

Romance is Murder: Bijoux Mystery Series Book 1

A dead diva, a rotten romance, and a town full of nosy neighbors...

Morgan Hart is home. A former homicide detective in Detroit, Morgan is back in her old hometown of Bijoux, Michigan to take over the reins of Sheriff from her dad, Able. The town has undergone quite a transformation since she lived here with new, kitschy shops along Main Street and a burgeoning tourist trade. Even the iconic pink Firefly Bed & Breakfast has jumped on the bandwagon and is hosting a romance writers' convention with some of the biggest names in the 'happily ever after' biz.

Morgan hopes to ease into her new job, new cottage, and new life – after all, Bijoux hasn't had a murder in a hundred years. But all of Morgan's plans go up in smoke when the biggest diva of the romance world is found dead.

As Morgan and her deputy, JJ Jones, begin their investigation, the townspeople have no qualms about telling her how to do her job, including Caleb Joseph, owner of the local bookstore who is far too nosy (and attractive) for Morgan's comfort.

With a murder to solve and the town in turmoil, Morgan will have to rely on her big city cop skills to catch a killer harboring a hate for happy endings.

Mystics are Murder: Bijoux Mystery Series Book 2

What do you do when your star murder witness only speaks 'Meow?'

Who could predict it would happen again? Morgan Hart didn't expect her first day as police captain of Bijoux, Michigan, the sleepy lakeside town where she grew up, would include a murder, even though that's just what happened. But with the killer behind bars, Morgan can take a breath and start painting her cozy cottage.

Or so she hopes.

When a fortune-telling mystic is found dead at Bijoux's Walk into the Light Psychic Gathering, Morgan and her deputy, JJ Jones, are called in to investigate. The trouble is Morgan's only witness is Griselda, a black cat with blood on her paws.

While every psychic in town claims to know what the cat 'knows,' Morgan relies on her own instincts to sniff out the suspects while dodging her conflicting feelings for local bookshop owner and town hunk, Caleb Joseph. And with her dad, Able's, upcoming wedding to Zoe Buffet, Bijoux's most famous clairvoyant and coffee cake queen, Morgan is under the gun to figure out which mystic is the murderer before the couple says I do.

Cupcakes are Murder: Bijoux Mystery Series Book 3

A cupcake conundrum, a culinary queen on the edge, and a cold-case killer on the loose...

Morgan Hart is settling into her job as police captain of Bijoux, the quaint and quirky tourist town nestled on the Lake Michigan shoreline. Murders have been solved, kittens have been rescued, and progress has been made in the renovation of her cozy cottage by the beach. Despite her grief and ongoing frustration over her husband's unsolved murder six years ago, Morgan hopes an overdue break in the case will finally lead to justice, even if it means exposing a betrayal that could leave her reeling.

Meanwhile, Morgan needs to keep a sharp eye on the upcoming Baker's Dozen Hometown Cupcake Bake-off and TV special hosted by British baking superstar Sassy McComas, aka The Queen of Cupcakes. Rumor has it, Queen Sass is secretly searching for a fresh face to host a new TV show and the competitors vying for the top spot include Bijoux's own pastry princess, Hannah Bellamy.

But when one of the top challengers in the Cupcake Bake-off turns up dead, Morgan has to sift through the evidence and stop the killer before they strike again and threaten to topple Queen Sass from her throne.

Pumpkins are Murder: Bijoux Mystery Series Book 4

A dead carver, dueling witches, and more tricks than treats...

Bijoux, Michigan is serious about Halloween.

Known as the most haunted town on the Lake Michigan shoreline, Bijoux hosts the annual Pumpkins and Poe Festival—the town's annual homage to Edgar Allan Poe and all things spooky. Pumpkin carvers from around the country flock to Bijoux, slicing and dicing their way into Halloween history. But when one of the carvers turns up dead with a jack-o-lantern on their head and a note with the word Nevermore scrawled in orange ink pinned to their apron, police captain Morgan Hart is called in to investigate.

After solving multiple murders at three previous Bijoux events, the beleaguered police captain steps into the fray once again, along with her down-in-the-dumps deputy, JJ Jones, recently ditched by his girlfriend, local cupcake maven, Hannah Bellamy. Meanwhile, Morgan's own "weak and weary" heart keeps getting tested by Caleb Joseph, owner of the Raven's Nest bookstore. The too-hot-for-his-own-good former Gothic Lit professor has made a hobby out of snooping around Morgan's cases.

It's up to Morgan to thwart various Halloween high-jinks around Bijoux while preventing the town from panicking as she tries to catch a killer who's turned "trick or treat" into the darkest diversion of all—murder.

Mistletoe is Murder: Bijoux Mystery Series Book 5

Skeletons with secrets, prohibition pirates, and holiday hijinks...

Morgan Hart is hoping for a boring Christmas. After eight months of murderous mayhem in her hometown of Bijoux, Michigan, she just wants to snuggle under a warm blanket in front of a cozy fire, with a good book, a hot chocolate (extra marshmallows of course), and Griselda purring beside her. She might even work up the nerve to ask Caleb Joseph over for dinner. Cal, the attractive owner of the Raven's Nest bookstore, has become a good friend since Morgan moved back home to take on the job of police captain.

A bestselling mystery author, Cal recently purchased the old Lawrence Mansion on the edge of town and plans to throw a big Christmas Eve bash. But Morgan's holiday plans—romantic and otherwise—go up in smoke when dark and shadowy secrets are revealed during the clean-up of the 19th century-built home. Can Morgan and Cal uncover the ghostly truth or are they destined for a disastrous deck-the-halls?

ORACLE DREAMS TRILOGY

Historical/Paranormal Time Travel Romance Series

Through the Mists of Time: Book One

London 1865…Valerie Sherwood Brooks has lived her entire life vicariously through books.

Due to a childhood accident, which left her with a permanent limp, Valerie has grown up under the watchful eye of her protective parents. When her banker father announces he's taking the family to Italy to look into an investment opportunity, Valerie is overjoyed at the prospect of leaving London for the excitement of exploring the ancient ruins of Pompeii.

But the romantic young woman who yearns for adventure is unprepared when an earthquake shatters their visit to the old city. Valerie is flung back in time to 79 A.D. where she's thrust into a world of intrigue and danger in the grand home of the darkly handsome, Christos Marcellus. As Valerie tries to keep her wits about her, she is torn between her growing and complicated feelings for Christos and the impending doom of the coming eruption of Vesuvius— knowing it will bring death and destruction.

Shadow Dreams: Book Two

In the village of Paran, in the peaceful plane of Keilah, lurks an evil bent on destruction.

Bethany M'Doro, a Healer and a Knower, possesses the unique ability to see into the past. Her gifts make her invaluable on Paran's archeological digs. The team's most recent discovery—charred bones and a wooden box with an ornate comb—sparks a vision of Eitel, an ancient cult known for stealing souls. Children's souls. A mysterious woman also appears in Bethany's vision, a woman named Elizabeth Jessup, who recently traveled through a portal from the Earth plane.

A widow, Bethany relies on her father to watch over her daughter Sarah, while she is on her expeditions. When Bethany returns home to Paran, her worst fear has come to pass. Sarah is missing along with several other children from the village.

Bethany realizes the resurrected cult of Eitel is responsible for abducting Sarah and the other young ones. And their leader is the traveler, Elizabeth Jessup. Bethany's visions lead her to the Earth plane, to Devil's Gate, Nevada in 1875, to enlist the help of Connor Jessup—Elizabeth's husband—a broken and embittered man.

Bethany now faces the greatest challenges of her life—heal Connor and convince him to travel back with her to Paran to unravel the secrets of Eitel and save Sarah and the other children.

Pagan Fire: Book Three

In the ancient village of Tintagel, Cornwall when old magic still illuminates the night sky, a young warrior embarks on a quest to reclaim his rightful place and the woman who haunts his dreams…

Dylan mac Connall survived the slaughter of his family ten years ago by a traitor to their clan. A young boy at the time, he was rescued by Kate, a wise witch woman who taught him the ways of magic and warned him of the peril that lays ahead if he chooses a path of revenge.

Raised in an abbey by the Sisters of Saint Columba, Maere cu Llwyr is ready to take her full vows and become a nun. But when a handsome warrior named Dylan arrives and claims to be her rightful betrothed, Maere is shocked and afraid of what her future will bring. A wee child when she was abducted from her village, Maere has blocked the memories of that horrific night. She has no recollection of the powerful ancient magic dormant inside her. Or of the childhood friend, who now stands before her, determined, to unlock both Maere's mind and her power.

As Maere and Dylan travel back to Tintagel, they must face the mercurial goddess Morrigu, dangerous Viking raiders, and the evil man who destroyed their families. Can Maere and Dylan survive the battles to come and find their way back home and to each other?

The Oracle Dreams Trilogy is also available as a Boxed Set at amazon.com.

NON-FICTION

Visit ReikiOne.com, PresenceandShadow.com, and/or SacredPriestess Journeys.com for more information.

Beginnings: ReikiOne First Degree Manual

This manual covers the basics of Reiki training and practice, including history, principles, hand positions, and treatment guidelines. Also included is a brief introduction to the chakras and using crystals with Reiki.

The Deeper Journey: ReikiOne Second Degree Manual

The ReikiOne Second Degree Manual includes the three symbols traditionally associated with this degree, explanations and their use, methods of distance healing, sending Reiki through time and space, combining symbols for greater effect, the chakra system, the human aura, and a suggested reading list.

Reiki Master: ReikiOne Third Degree Manual Part A by Teri Barnett, Reiki Master Teacher

This book contains the 4th symbol, its use for Reiki treatments, a discussion of what it means to be a Reiki Master, and how to use crystal grids with Reiki.

Reiki Master Teacher: ReikiOne Third Degree Manual Part B

The Master Teacher Manual contains all the information your students need for stepping into Reiki Master Teacher - A review of the 4th symbol (plus additional data on this symbol), the 5th symbol for attunements, attunement instructions (individual and group), methods and ethics of teaching, getting in touch with your inner teacher, marketing ideas, an extensive reading list, and much more.

The Reiki Teacher's Handbook

A composite of all the ReikiOne Manuals, the Reiki Teacher's Handbook takes your teaching a step further. This book provides you with all the tools you'll need to teach Reiki. Written from the experienced perspective of a master Teacher of the Usui Shiki Ryoho method, you'll find this book adapts easily to other forms of Reiki and can grow with you as you progress on your teaching path.

www.ingramcontent.com/pod-product-compliance
Lightning Source LLC
Chambersburg PA
CBHW020123180626
46812CB00006B/2707